WRITTEN IN ink

CARRIE ANN
NEW YORK TIMES BESTSELLING AUTHOR
RYAN

WRITTEN IN INK - SPECIAL EDITION
MONTGOMERY INK

CARRIE ANN RYAN

WRITTEN IN INK

A Montgomery Ink Novel

By
Carrie Ann Ryan

Written in Ink
A Montgomery Ink Novel
By: Carrie Ann Ryan
© 2015 Carrie Ann Ryan

This book is a work of fiction. Names, characters, places, and incidents either are products of the author's imagination or are used fictitiously. Any resemblance to actual events, locales or persons, living or dead, is entirely coincidental.
No part of this book can be reproduced in any form or by electronic or mechanical means including information storage and retrieval systems, without the express written permission of the author. The only exception is by a reviewer who may quote short excerpts in a review.

All content warnings are listed on the book page for this book on my website.

NO AI TRAINING: Without in any way limiting the author's [and publisher's] exclusive rights under copyright, any use of this publication to "train" generative artificial intelligence (AI) technologies to generate text is expressly prohibited. The author reserves all rights to license uses of this work for generative AI training and development of machine learning language models.

PRAISE FOR CARRIE ANN RYAN....

"Count on Carrie Ann Ryan for emotional, sexy, character driven stories that capture your heart!" – Carly Phillips, NY Times bestselling author

"Carrie Ann Ryan's romances are my newest addiction! The emotion in her books captures me from the very beginning. The hope and healing hold me close until the end. These love stories will simply sweep you away." ~ NYT Bestselling Author Deveny Perry

"Carrie Ann Ryan writes the perfect balance of sweet and heat ensuring every story feeds the soul." - Audrey Carlan, #1 New York Times Bestselling Author

"Carrie Ann Ryan never fails to draw readers in with passion, raw sensuality, and characters that pop off the page. Any book by Carrie Ann is an absolute treat." – New York Times Bestselling Author J. Kenner

"Carrie Ann Ryan knows how to pull your heartstrings and make your pulse pound! Her wonderful Redwood Pack series will draw you in and keep you reading long into the night. I can't wait to see what comes next with the new generation, the Talons. Keep them coming, Carrie Ann!" –Lara Adrian, New York Times bestselling author of CRAVE THE NIGHT

"With snarky humor, sizzling love scenes, and brilliant, imaginative worldbuilding, The Dante's Circle series reads as if Carrie Ann Ryan peeked at my personal wish list!" – NYT Bestselling Author, Larissa Ione

"Carrie Ann Ryan writes sexy shifters in a world full of passionate happily-ever-afters." – *New York Times* Bestselling Author Vivian Arend

"Carrie Ann's books are sexy with characters you can't help but love from page one. They are heat and heart blended to perfection." *New York Times* Bestselling Author Jayne Rylon

Carrie Ann Ryan's books are wickedly funny and deliciously hot, with plenty of twists to keep you guessing. They'll keep you up all night!" USA Today Bestselling Author Cari Quinn

"Once again, Carrie Ann Ryan knocks the Dante's Circle series out of the park. The queen of hot, sexy, enthralling paranormal romance, Carrie Ann is an author not to miss!" *New York Times* bestselling Author Marie Harte

DEDICATION

To those who are still looking for who they are; who they were.
You'll find that person...or maybe you already have.
Just breathe. We're here. We promise.

WRITTEN IN INK

NYT Bestselling Author Carrie Ann Ryan continues her Montgomery Ink series with the quiet Montgomery, as he finds his match in the woman with a fiery passion and a past full of secrets.

Autumn Minor is light on her feet and a bare memory for most people she meets. She does her best to blend in everywhere she lives, even if it's only for a short period of time. Making sure no one truly notices her is the only way she's survived this long. When she meets Griffin Montgomery, she's afraid she won't be able to let go when it's time to run.

He's her boss for only a few weeks, yet they know the attraction between them is wrong. Neither of them are made for the long haul when it comes to love and romance. When the demons from Autumn's past find her and put both their lives at risk, Griffin will stop at nothing to protect her—even if he might lose her in the end, no matter what.

CHAPTER ONE

Sometimes there was nothing better than a well-worn pair of jeans. Okay, perhaps it would be more accurate to say there was nothing better than a well-worn pair of jeans encasing a very tight butt. Especially as the owner of said butt worked around a construction site.

Autumn Minor leaned against the side of the truck and crossed her arms over her chest, appreciating the view before she had to start work. At least five different men worked around her, bending over and lifting heavy things, using their large thighs and flexing nice butts. It was as if she'd entered the mecca of sexy men in jeans.

She really needed to stop by the Montgomery Inc. construction sites more often. Maybe standing back and drooling over men was a bit sexist, but she'd also seen the appreciative glances from who she assumed were the single and willing men on the site. She didn't whistle or holler at them, so really, as far as she was concerned, she was one step ahead of the game when it came to checking out construction workers.

"Are you checking out my fiancé's very fine butt?" Meghan Montgomery-Warren, soon to be Montgomery-Dodd, asked as she leaned against the truck next to Autumn, her long legs crossed one in front of the other, muddy boots looking well worn but cared for.

Autumn stretched from the truck, her back a little tight, and pulled her long auburn hair back into a ponytail. "Pretty much. Got a problem with that?" She winked over her shoulder at her friend, and Meghan rolled her eyes.

"No problem at all. As long as all you're doing is looking and not touching." Meghan's teeth bit into her lip as she tilted her head, presumably checking out Luc's...assets. "Damn, I love that man's butt. Well, I just love him in general."

Autumn grinned; ignoring that little ache inside that she hoped wasn't jealousy. Not over Luc, of course, but of the idea that someone could love another with that much emotion and not be scared by it. The depth of heart and soul displayed on her friend's face surprised her, though it shouldn't have. Meghan looked so freaking in love that Autumn's teeth hurt with the sweetness of it. The look in Meghan's eyes when she thought Luc wasn't looking made any amount of discomfort worth it, though. Her friend was well and truly loved. And after Meghan's first abusive and disastrous marriage, she deserved all of that and more.

"You two are perfect together," Autumn said. She put her hands in her pockets, trying to warm up in Denver's winter weather. It hadn't snowed in a couple of days, so of course the foot of white powder and ice they'd gotten during the last storm had already melted thanks to Colorado's lovely weather patterns. But it still wasn't warm enough for her. She preferred more temperate weather. Maybe the next place she lived wouldn't have such cold winters.

She held in a sigh. Thinking about the next stop in her never-ending nomadic life didn't tend to put a smile on her face.

Enough of those thoughts.

She liked Denver, even if the weather never made sense or stayed the same throughout the day. She'd learned to dress in layers—and lots of them. She also liked the Montgomerys. She didn't know how it had happened, but somehow, she'd been invited into the fold and became, if not one of them, at least part of their periphery crew.

Meghan brushed her shoulder against Autumn's and smiled. The two of them were around the same height, so thankfully, Autumn didn't have to look up like she did with so many others at the site. It wasn't that she was short—she was average—but the men on the site were all gigantic specimens of sexy men. Hence the firm butts in tight jeans and their need for appreciation.

"It's about lunchtime. I know some of the guys wanted to head to the café near here," Meghan said. "You want to join us, or did you bring your lunch?"

Autumn shook her head then winced. Shaking her head where there was more than one question involved usually led to misunderstandings. Considering she spent her life studying situations and people, she was usually better at that. There was just something about Denver—or maybe it was the Montgomerys—that made her feel...off-kilter.

"I didn't bring my lunch, and I'd love to join you if you have room." She shivered a bit, bouncing from one foot to the other. "Don't the guys usually bring their meals so they don't have to take so much time off the site?"

Meghan folded her arms over her chest, presumably to stay warm. "Yeah, but there's a cold front coming in with the possibility of a storm, so we're bringing things in early."

"I knew there was a reason I'm cold down to my bones." She swore her teeth chattered, but it wasn't *that* cold.

Meghan rolled her eyes. "I think that has more to do with you being a Denver newbie. Anyway, it's hard for the guys in the winter. Of course, it's hard in the heat of the summer, too. But since they don't want to get caught up in a foot of snow, we're packing up."

Autumn lowered her brows. "I still don't know why you need my help, or even why *you're* working outside in the winter. You work with landscapes."

The Montgomery family had their hands in many pots when it came to professions, but a large part of them worked at either Montgomery Inc.—the construction company—or Montgomery Ink—the tattoo shop. The latter, ironically, was where she'd met the Montgomerys in the first place. Now, Autumn worked with the other arm of the family business. Meghan hadn't always been part of the construction branch of the family, but once she'd divorced and found her way, she joined and dug elbows deep in dirt and plants.

"I don't do as much in the winter when it comes to actual planting since the ground is usually too wet or too frozen. But there is always planning, upkeep, and other things I can do. And I need help because I'm learning to not do everything on my own." She winked. "Luc doesn't want me to wear myself out."

He probably wanted to wear his fiancée out on his own, but Autumn wasn't about to say that. From the heated look in Meghan's eyes when she looked in Luc's direction, her friend's mind had already gone there anyway.

As if she'd conjured him from her look alone, Luc glanced over his shoulder and smiled. He nodded at two of the other guys he had been working with and strolled over to Meghan and Autumn.

"I felt your eyes on me. That mean you're ready for lunch?" He lifted a dark brow, and Meghan laughed. She held out a hand, and Luc took it before tugging and bringing her to his chest.

Autumn held in a little sigh at the sight.

"I was just admiring your form," Meghan said softly before kissing his chin.

Luc lowered his mouth to hers and gently brushed a

kiss across her lips. "I can bend over again if you'd like a better look."

"Maybe later," Meghan murmured, sinking into her man's hold.

This time, Autumn didn't bother holding in her sigh.

"Those two are so sickeningly sweet, my teeth ache," Wes Montgomery said as he came to Autumn's side.

"You just don't like seeing your sister making out with your electrician," Tabby Collins said as she made her way to the group with Decker and Storm on her heels.

"True enough," Storm Montgomery said as he tilted his chin toward Autumn. The man was built, bearded, and did that sexy chin tilt thing just right. She might have wanted to explore that sexy edge about him, but since she worked with him *and* she didn't feel an overwhelming urge to let him see her naked, she didn't act on it.

Of course, *all* the Montgomerys were damn sexy. She'd been Meghan's neighbor before working with them, so she'd met most of them at one point or another. And she hadn't found an ugly one in the bunch. There were eight siblings, though, so it wasn't easy to keep them all straight. Maybe she should number them or something. Wes and Storm were twins, and two of the eldest Montgomerys. They owned and operated Montgomery Inc.—with Wes being the lead foreman for all projects and Storm being the lead architect.

Apparently, they even hired sexy. Tabby was their head receptionist, and in Autumn's opinion, the glue that held them all together. Though she wasn't sure the other woman knew that. When Autumn had first started hanging out with them, she thought Tabby and Wes might have had a thing going on, but now that she knew them better, she rethought that.

Decker, their lead contractor, tilted his head at the loving couple in front of them. "I thought you weren't going to let them make out at the job site anymore."

Luc and Meghan each held a hand out, flipping the group off even as they kept their eyes on each other.

"Considering you make out with *our* sister whenever she visits, you don't have much room to speak," Wes said dryly. Decker had recently married the youngest Montgomery, Miranda. He'd been a part of the family long before that, however; though Autumn wasn't sure of the exact specifics.

"And I will keep on making out with her as long as I damn well please," Decker said before running his hand over his beard. His ink flexed over his muscles as he did, and Autumn couldn't help but admire the work. Each of the Montgomerys and their loved ones had ink—some more than others—and Autumn was pretty sure the two tattoo artists in the family, Austin and Maya, were the ones who had done it. As if either of those two would let anyone else touch their family's skin. In fact, Autumn was going to find it hard to have anyone else do her ink once she moved away. But it wasn't as if she could afford to come back just for Maya's or Austin's talent. As much as she loved their work, it wasn't worth their safety.

She forced that thought out of her mind. This wasn't the time or the place to worry about things like that. Though, in all honesty, she was *always* worried about that.

"Anyway, once the couple is done, we're going to lunch," Tabby said with a smile. "Are you planning on joining us? I know you don't work with Meghan full-time, so you probably have other plans."

Autumn shrugged. "I get work where I can," she said vaguely. Always vaguely. "I'm hungry. Food sounds good." She shivered again. "And if we could eat indoors with a nice heater and maybe a roaring fire, I'd be even happier."

"It's not that cold, cupcake," Storm said dryly.

"Don't call me cupcake." She raised a brow at him,

but he didn't even bother to look repentant. Damn Montgomery men.

She looked back over at Meghan, who had her hand lightly resting on Luc's shoulder with a sad look in her eyes. Autumn held back another shiver, this one having nothing to do with the cold. She remembered the first time she'd met Luc, though she knew he didn't. He'd been on the floor, covered in his own blood, Meghan's hand on his shoulder then, as well. But that time, his fiancée had been trying to keep him alive.

He'd been shot, and Autumn couldn't do anything to help him but try to keep Meghan calm. Others said that had been enough, but she wasn't sure. She could still remember the screams…though she wasn't sure if they were Meghan's or her own.

She swallowed the bile that rose in her throat and tried to shake off the memories that were best forgotten.

"You weren't lifting anything, right?" Meghan asked, worry in her tone.

"He better not have been," Wes snapped.

Luc shook his head. "I only bent over to point something out to another person earlier. I'm just observing, and I'm not even working full days yet." He cupped Meghan's face. "I promise."

"Good." Meghan rose up on her tiptoes and kissed him again. This time it was Tabby who sighed.

"I know, right?" Autumn said to the other woman.

Tabby snorted. "You should see it when Austin has Sierra, Shep is with Shea, Morgan gets with Callie, Decker has Miranda, and now...Luc with Meghan. It's like love and heat and romance all rolled up in ink and shivers."

Autumn smiled at the thought. "I don't think I've met a few of those you mentioned, but I can guess how all of that in one place could almost be too much."

Tabby shrugged. "I think once the rest of the Montgomerys settle down, Harry and Marie will be in grandbaby and new family heaven." She winced as she said that, but Wes rubbed her shoulder. "Sorry."

"It's okay," Wes said. "Dad's getting better." From the way he'd ground that out, it was as if it were a forced hope, not an actual fact. But Autumn wasn't about to comment on that. "No use tiptoeing around it."

Ah, that was right. Harry Montgomery was going through chemo and radiation for cancer. The mention of the heaven of such a perfect future, or even just the word heaven like that might bother some of them. Sometimes just the casual word here and there could hurt more than intended.

"Okay, enough of the making out," Storm muttered. "Let's haul it in and head to Taboo."

Autumn smiled. She *loved* Taboo. Their friend Hailey ran the small café that was located right off the 16th Street Mall in downtown Denver. Plus, a side door to Montgomery Ink connected it with the café so the family could walk back and forth between the two places easily. Since the job site was in Edgewater, they were only fifteen minutes away. *And,* Montgomery Ink had parking in the back lot. Not an easy thing to come by.

"Come on, then," Wes said, wrapping his arm around Tabby's shoulders. She rolled her eyes and took a step back, poking him in the ribs as she did so.

"I'll drive myself, thank you very much. I need to head home instead of back to the office after lunch."

Wes and Storm both frowned, looking very much like the twins they were. "Why?" they asked in unison.

Tabby raised a brow. "I have my own reasons, and I told you both last week that I plan on working from home in the afternoons. Now let's go to lunch. I'm starved." With that very cryptic statement, Tabby bounced away, her hand moving frantically over her tablet as she did so. How the woman didn't trip while multitasking like that, Autumn would never know.

"Oh, stop being pains in the asses," Decker

muttered. "Tabby works her ass off. You don't need to know *everything* she does."

"But what if she needs help?" Wes asked, his gaze on Tabby. Again, Autumn would have thought that look meant something more at one point, but now she saw the same type of brotherly worry there he had for Meghan, Maya, and Miranda.

"Then she'll ask for it," Autumn said simply. Just because *she* didn't know how to ask for help, didn't mean that was the case for most people. "Tabby seems like she trusts you guys enough to ask for help if she needs it. Now I'm freaking freezing. Can we please go? Or are we going to stand here and look like sad puppies while the lovebirds make out some more and Tabby ends up alone and warm at Taboo eating *all* the food?"

The twins huffed then did that chin tilt thing once again before heading off to their vehicles. Since Autumn had ridden in with Meghan, she jumped in the back seat of the truck, knowing Luc would rather sit up front. He wasn't quite cleared to drive yet since his shoulder was still technically healing, and Autumn knew that bugged him to no end. Hence why she didn't tease him. She wasn't sure she would ever be able to get the image of him lying pale on the ground in a pool of his own blood out of her brain; no matter how hard she tried.

Though perhaps that was a good thing.

It was a stark reminder that no matter how hard someone tried, their past could return with a vengeance and hurt those around them. That's why it was a good idea to never get too close.

She pressed her lips together as Meghan drove them to Taboo. It would do Autumn well to remember not to get too close. Or at least not get closer than she already had. She knew the others wondered about her and had probably figured out that she was always vague when she talked about what she did and why she was in Denver. It wasn't as if she could actually tell them, but it was starting to wear on her that she *couldn't* say anything.

They pulled into the parking lot and headed into Taboo without much fuss thankfully. And since it was technically after the lunch rush, the place wasn't too busy. Hailey stood behind the counter, talking to one of her customers. Her thick blond bob shifted from side to side as she shook her head. Her blunt bangs and bright red lips made her look like she should have come from the age of starlets and bombshells, instead of working at a Denver café in the twenty-first century.

Hailey's eyes lit up when she saw them, and Autumn gave a little wave before sitting down at the long table in the corner. She took the seat closest to the end and kept her back to the wall and her eyes on the door. It was instinct to sit like that, and she hoped no one would notice that she tried to sit there—or in places like it—every time.

She ended up sitting by Tabby, who also sat next to Meghan. The boys took up the other side of the table, with Luc sitting at the head next to his fiancée. That left one more chair next to Autumn, but since they weren't expecting anyone else to join them, it seemed she'd have some space.

Hailey came over with a smile and a roll of her eyes. She handed out waters to each of them, balancing her heavy tray like it weighed nothing. "Couldn't keep away from me?"

"You know it, sugar," Storm drawled, and Hailey snorted.

"The usual coffees for everyone?" Hailey asked.

"Yes, please," they all said in unison. Kind of creepy, but Autumn liked feeling part of a unit. Plus, Hailey knew *exactly* how to make each of their lattes, cappuccinos, and chicory coffees. That was just one of the many reasons they all came here so much. Hailey smiled then bounced away to get their drinks.

"Don't say things like that around Sloane, or you're likely to end up with a black eye," Wes muttered.

"Like what?" Storm asked before taking a drink of his water. "I was just being polite."

"And don't mention Sloane around Hailey," Tabby said softly. "You know that's a sore subject."

Autumn frowned but didn't voice the questions she wanted to ask. Everyone had been friends for much longer than she'd been in town, so it wasn't as if she knew *everything* that was going on. But sometimes it was as if she were on the outside looking in with her nose pressed up against the glass.

Of course, wasn't that what she wanted?

It was the safest place to be.

It had to be.

"How's Alex doing?" Tabby asked in a whisper as the guys talked amongst themselves.

Autumn leaned into Tabby as she spoke to Meghan about one of the other Montgomery brothers. Alex was in rehab after having a breakdown at Decker and Miranda's wedding. Her heart hurt for the man and his troubles, but at least he was most likely getting help now.

Meghan met Autumn's eyes, then Tabby's. "He's okay. I think." She worried her lip, and Luc reached out and gripped her hand without her even having to look at him.

"He won't let us see him," Wes said, letting them

know he was indeed paying attention to the other side of the table.

"He will, though," Meghan said firmly. "We're family."

"Damn straight," Storm added.

Autumn leaned back in her chair and pressed her lips together. Damn, she missed her family. Missed the way things used to be, though she knew they would never be that way again. Change and circumstances had seen fit to make that happen.

"Why the long faces?" a voice said from her side.

She looked up—way up—at the sexiest man she'd ever seen. And considering the hot as hell at her table right then, that was saying something. He had a day's growth of beard on his firm jaw, and cheekbones that looked like they could cut glass. He was seriously pretty in a ruggedly handsome, I'm-in-a-bad-mood-so-don't-fuck-with-me sort of way. His hair was dark brown like the rest of the Montgomerys, and he'd cut it shorter on the sides but kept it long and spiked on top. From the way it went every which way, it also looked like he ran his fingers through it often. His dark blue eyes were also a Montgomery trait, but for some reason, she couldn't help but feel like there was something...*more* to them than merely blue. Though she wasn't sure what just then.

He looked like he'd rushed to put on a white button up shirt, but didn't bother to button the bottom one or tuck it in. He'd also rolled up his sleeves, showing his tan skin and intricate ink. She wanted to lick up every inch of him, and from the way he looked at her, he knew it.

She cleared her throat as Tabby nudged her.

"Autumn? You okay?" Decker asked, giving her a knowing look. She'd have flipped him off, but she didn't want to deal with any more questions about her reaction to the man in front of her.

He was a Montgomery, and since she'd met the rest of them except for Alex, who was in rehab, this had to be Griffin. The writer. The mysterious one, who had so far evaded her. Even in the hospital when she'd visited Meghan and Luc she hadn't met him; and she wasn't sure if that was a good thing or not.

This reaction was surely not good for her.

"I'm fine." She took a quick sip of her water since her voice sounded a bit too throaty for her. "What's up?"

Storm winked. "Well, cupcake, we were just introducing you to Griffin, but you seemed lost in space."

"Don't call me cupcake," she said absently, then turned back to Griffin and held out her hand. "Nice to meet you, Griffin."

He clenched his jaw then gripped her hand in his own. She refused to think about the heat of his palm or the shock of flesh against flesh. It was nothing. Just a momentary lapse in judgment when it came to her thoughts.

"Cupcake?" he asked as he pulled away and took the last seat at the table—the seat closest to her, of course.

"Storm is a dead man who happens to think he's funny," she said dryly, pulling her eyes from his too handsome face.

"I'm sure—" Griffin whispered.

Hailey came at that exact moment and handed them their drinks and took their orders, saving Autumn from having to deal with whatever the fuck had just happened. She'd met sexy men before, so it wasn't like this was new. But she sure hadn't had *that* reaction before. Maybe she was just hungry and lost in her own thoughts.

Because there was no way she would get with a Montgomery. Not when they were the only ones to hold her close when she walked through the shadows of her life. And she would be leaving soon anyway. Looking too closely at a man who made her brain and body act as if she'd been plugged into an electrical socket wouldn't help.

"Nice to meet you, Autumn," Griffin whispered in her ear. She held back a shiver at the feel of his breath on her neck.

This could be a problem.

"Or maybe I should call you Fall."

She blinked at him, her jaw dropping at the lame joke.

Or maybe it wouldn't be a problem at all.

CHAPTER TWO

Writing a book was not for the sane of mind. Griffin Montgomery contemplated banging his head on his desk, but he'd done that a few times before, and all it had left him with was a headache and the beginning of a bruise—not so much with the words of wisdom needed to write a book. Or at least what he qualified as wisdom with his work.

He ran his hand through his hair once again and frowned.

When exactly had he last washed it?

He'd worked out two days ago. He thought. Maybe. And he's showered after that—because not doing so wasn't an option after a hard workout. But had he even thought of taking the extra time to jump in the shower since? Showering took time. Standing under the water and scrubbing down took minutes that could better be used to write. If he didn't immediately sit down at his desk or in his thinking chair, he wouldn't work. He'd find something else to do.

So when had he last showered?

Well, shit. If he had to ask that question, he was probably a day or two late in getting clean.

Griffin Montgomery was one hell of a prize.

He ran his hands over his face. Ah, yes, it *had* been two days ago because it had also been two days since he'd made a complete ass of himself in the middle of Taboo with Meghan's friend Autumn.

What on earth had possessed him to call her Fall? Of all the juvenile jokes in all the most immature lands possible, he'd gone with *Fall*.

He banged his head on the desk despite his earlier rumblings of not wanting to hurt his brain. He was already pretty brain-dead at this point if the words coming out of his mouth and *not* on the page were any indication.

It wasn't as if he hadn't heard of Fall—*Autumn*—before. She'd been slowly weaving herself into the Montgomery clan, member by member, for a little while now. He just hadn't had the chance to actually meet her. When Luc had been in the hospital, Griffin's arrival apparently hadn't coincided with hers. The guys had described her somewhat in casual conversation, but damn...

They hadn't mentioned the fact that she was knock down gorgeous.

Plump lips and plumper hips, she looked like a damn siren fully prepared to call men to their deaths just for a sweet taste of her. With her auburn hair, she effusively fit the part of a sultry water nymph ready to tempt the chastest of sailors. She had a spattering of freckles on her nose and shoulders, and he wanted to see where else they would dot her ivory skin.

He groaned and adjusted his cock behind his fly. Damn it. He didn't have time to get a hard-on for one of Meghan's friends. Especially one who looked at him like she wanted to simultaneously study him under a microscope and turn her back on him in disinterest.

Autumn intrigued him.

And that could be very dangerous for a writer.

Especially a writer who was officially behind on deadline.

Griffin let out another groan, but this time it had nothing to do with being horny and everything to do with being a failure at the one thing he thought he could do. All of the Montgomerys were talented. They were artists, scholars, teachers, nurturers, and so much more.

He was merely a creator of worlds, but he was damn good at it.

Or at least he used to be.

Now he was behind on one deadline and looking in the face of another. Why the hell had he tried to write two series? Most thriller writers only wrote one. They branded themselves as that series—or at least that main character—and kept going for as long as the publishing house let them.

Griffin had to be different.

He had two long-running series that had both hit lists and did reasonably well. He wasn't one of the big names in the business, but he was respectable—considering his age. He also usually loved putting one series aside and digging into another. It kept him fresh. And it was like going back and visiting an old friend once he got back into the first series.

He put out two to three books a year, which was actually quite a lot compared to some. But damn, he sometimes felt like it was twenty books a year, instead of the amount he actually did.

He was *tired*.

He also had no idea what to do with his current book. His characters weren't talking to him, and damn it, they weren't even sitting in the same room with him. Instead, he had a feeling that both sets of characters were off together on vacation, hiding from him and laughing in his general direction.

His series weren't actually connected, but he liked to think that since each was set in a different city, they were in the same world. Maybe his two main characters, Jensen and Will, met up for coffee every once in a while. Of course, after the last thing Griffin had done to Jensen, he wasn't sure the character would ever want to speak to *him* again.

He didn't write romance. His books were ongoing and never had the required happily ever after, but Jensen *had* been in a serious relationship for the five books Griffin had worked on. In the most recent release, Starr, Jensen's serious girlfriend and soon-to-be-fiancée had died thanks to a serial killer bent on torturing Jensen.

The readers simultaneously loved and hated Griffin for the death and the way Jensen had broken under the calamity. Griffin hadn't gone into writing the book with that kind of pain in mind, but he'd seen what needed to happen in his mind and knew it had to be done.

Will, his other main character, had never had a serious relationship and had no real family so his emotional arc was quite different and put Griffin's head into a new space. Griffin would be starting that book next.

He just had to finish Jensen's new book first.

Only he had no idea how to do that.

The fact that both of his main characters were in a state of flux when it came to relationships and how they interacted with the world because of that should have told Griffin a bit about himself.

But he didn't want to hear it.

He saved his almost blank page just in case and pushed back from his desk, rolling his wrists as he did. They were starting to ache something fierce, and he figured he was well on his way to carpal tunnel if he didn't start taking care of himself.

He looked around at the mess of papers covering his room and the empty coffee cups and processed foods littering every surface.

Perhaps taking care of himself should lead to other areas of his life, as well.

Only now he wanted some sour patch kids and another cup of coffee because that would help him get a move on with his book. Sugar and caffeine were a writer's fuel. He didn't write drunk and edit sober as the memes claimed Hemmingway had once said, but maybe he should add a bit of drinking to his work.

Maybe that would help.

He thought back to his brother and the pain Alex was in at the moment, and Griffin immediately wanted to kick himself.

Drinking wouldn't help him. It never helped anyone. So maybe he needed to find his words and his will to write in other ways. Thoughts of Autumn and those delicious curves filled his mind and he groaned. Getting laid *might* help him clear his head, but it wouldn't be with Autumn. Griffin knew his three sisters well enough to know that if he dared to touch any of their friends, he'd end up with a bloody lip thanks to Maya, a punch in the gut courtesy of Miranda, and a glower to end all glowers from Meghan.

Damn sisters knew exactly where to draw blood.

He put his hands on his hips and looked around his office, ignoring the mess as he always did. He'd deal with the clutter once he finished his book. Of course, he said that after each book, and after each one, he got just a bit messier and a tad more desperate. At one point, he'd hired a cleaning service but had let them go after they kept interrupting his work.

Since he lived alone and didn't have anyone to rely on him when it came to being taken care of, he worked on his own schedule. So the service hadn't been able to pin down a time that would be good to show up and start the deep clean. After the third time of Griffin freaking out and yelling, they'd cancelled the service for him.

His family didn't know the exact details of how it had ended, but he knew they were disappointed that he couldn't function as a civilized person in society.

Well, fuck that. He was a writer. He didn't have to be civilized.

And look at that, he had a new tagline for the website his editor had wanted him to update a year ago.

He honestly wasn't *that* much of a loser. He went on dates when he felt like it and made it to family dinners and other events. Every few weeks he threw away most of the trash in his house, and up until recently, he'd been on top of his job and all that came with it. Only it turned out that after a few books, writing wasn't just writing anymore. He had to deal with...people.

Yes.

People.

He might look like a people person, considering he could smile and have fun once he was outside his home, but he'd rather be alone and confined to his thinking chair with a good book. Or, preferably, *writing* a good book.

He didn't have time to deal with social media, book tours, contracts, and other important things that came with being a writer, but he still did what he could with them. Most people in his line of work after his kind of success had a personal assistant or team that could help him with some of that, but he'd never felt the need to hire another person. He could do what he had to. Alone. He didn't need anyone else.

He looked around at his dirty room and thought of his lack of book, his outdated website, the stack of letters he knew were in his PO Box that he hadn't checked in four months, and various other things that he knew he was sorely behind on and cursed.

Maybe he wasn't handling it all.

Maybe he wasn't handling any of it.

But damn it, he didn't *want* to rely on another person. Why couldn't he just write what his characters needed and call it a day? Since when did writing become *work*?

Probably around the time he'd gotten his first advance and figured out that writing could earn him a living rather than just fill endless notebooks under his bed.

Of course if he could just *write* like he wanted to, would letting writing become fun and not work actually happen? The blank pages staring at him and judging were evidence that maybe he wasn't as good as he thought he was. Maybe he sucked ass and needed to go into the family business.

Of course, he couldn't draw for shit, and though he loved getting ink, he wasn't a fan of blood. So, joining Austin and Maya at their tattoo shop was out. And then there was that one time with the saw that shall never be mentioned again so he wouldn't be joining the twins and the crew at the construction company either. He'd already said he didn't much like people; so becoming a teacher where he'd work with little ones and Miranda wouldn't work. He could take a decent photograph, but he didn't have the talent Alex did when it came to being a photographer, so Griffin was pretty much screwed when it came to joining one of the family businesses.

He loved writing. He really did.

Or perhaps, he loved having written. It was the writing that sucked.

Hard.

"Knock knock!"

Griffin turned on his heel at his mother's voice at the front door and again wondered why he'd given his parents the key to his home. All of the Montgomery kids had in case of emergencies, and usually, his parents knocked and even called ahead before coming over. However, his mother knew him well. Knew him enough to realize that he probably wouldn't have answered the door if he were in his writing cave. It was a bad habit, but he didn't think he was about to stop it any time soon.

He looked over his shoulder at his mess of an office and knew the rest of his house wasn't faring much better. It hadn't been quite this bad in a while, but this was a hard book and an even tougher deadline.

He was a thirty-something-year-old man and was still worried about how his mother would react to seeing the mess he'd made in his own home. He wasn't sure the bedroom he'd shared with his brothers in the past had been this bad, but hell; this wasn't going to end well.

"Come in," he said dryly as he made his way into the living room. He stopped short when he saw that his mother wasn't alone.

The M&Ms were with her—Maya, Miranda, and Meghan. The only Montgomery woman missing was Sierra, but he figured she was home with the new baby.

When most of the women in his life showed up unannounced with scowls on their faces and hands on their hips, it couldn't end well for Griffin.

"Seriously, Griffin?" Maya clicked her tongue ring against her teeth and raised her brow. The ring there glittered under the sunlight peeking through his dark blinds.

He stuffed his hands in his pockets and leaned back on his heels. He was big, bearded, inked, and could fight with the best of them, but damn, his mom and sisters knew how to make him feel like he was a kid again. Just two words and a look and he knew he was in deep shit.

"Why are you here?" he asked, tired already.

"Is that any way to greet your mother?" Marie Montgomery asked with a smile. She opened her arms and he shuffled toward her, picking her up in a tight hug. He may be in trouble, but he wasn't about to say no to a hug from her.

"Hi, Mom," he mumbled and kissed the top of her head.

"That's better," she said as she patted his back. "Now, we're here for a reason, though we do enjoy seeing you."

He stood back and raised his brow at Meghan and Miranda, who hadn't spoken, but had similarly raised brows and side smiles on their faces like his mother.

"I figured you didn't stop by en masse just to shoot the shit."

"Language," Marie snapped with a smile.

He rolled his eyes at Miranda, who put her hand over her mouth to presumably hold back a laugh. Marie Montgomery cursed more than they did, but she still had fun parenting her kids when she could.

"So, what's up?" he asked, trying not to meet Miranda's eyes. If he did, he'd break out in a laugh, and he had a feeling his mom wouldn't like that.

"You're a mess, Grif," Meghan said softly.

He winced. "And this is different than usual, how?"

Miranda snorted. "You don't even want to deny that you're a mess."

He held his hands out and looked around the room. Clothes and dirty dishes littered every surface. Dust had piled up to the point he was pretty sure the dirt had run along with his plot bunnies and created hybrid creatures of doom. He was fairly certain the only things he had in his fridge were old eggs, some butter, and the beer Storm and Wes had left last week. Actually, he may have finished the beer the night before.

"Griffin, honey, you need help." His mother sighed but didn't try to help him clean up. She'd stopped doing that ages ago, and he was glad for it. He might be a slob on deadline, but it wasn't his mother's job to clean up after him. She had enough to deal with without including his mess of a life.

"I tried to hire cleaning services before and it didn't work out. I'll clean up after I finish my book. I promise."

Maya huffed. "You always clean up and eat well again after you finish a book. It's your MO. But it's different this time. You're behind on your deadline."

He took a step back, his eyes wide. "How the hell did you know that?"

"The twins told us," Meghan answered. He raised a brow. "You were drunk and mentioned it to them the last time you hung out. Really, I didn't know beer loosened your tongue like that. Anyway, I know I used to come over and help out when I could, but I can't anymore. None of us can."

Way to make him feel like a loser. "I never asked you to help me out, but I've always been grateful for it. Now, why don't you tell me why you're really here and stop harping on me for being who I am."

"Oh, shut up," Marie said. "We're here to help, and you are just going to have to deal. I know you like doing everything on your own, but you shouldn't have to."

"So we're stepping in."

Griffin frowned, a sense of something wrong climbing up his back. "You just said you weren't."

"We won't be helping personally, but we will help in a way," his mother said slowly. He opened his mouth to speak, but she held up her hand. "Let me finish. You are a grown man and I understand that. You work your ass off and do things with words that I've never thought of. You are one of my babies and bright stars. But you don't know how to ask for help. In fact, I'm pretty sure none of my kids do. Maybe that's my fault, but at least you're independent, right?"

"Mom..." he whispered.

"Shush. Now, where was I? Oh, yes, you are a brilliant writer, Griffin. Your books do well, and you have an amazing presence. But you are behind on everything else. I know you're behind on your words as well, and that's got to be a kick in the pants. So, what we're going to do is help you."

"You said that before, but I don't understand what you mean."

"We've hired you a personal assistant," Maya added.

His gaze snapped to his sisters. "What the fuck? You know I need to have a hand in that. You can't just randomly hire someone for me that will be a part of my life and work."

"We can and we did," Miranda said simply. "You'll like her."

"Her?"

"Yes, her," Meghan added. "She'll be here to help you clean and cook since you're beyond doing that. Though you might want to learn to take care of yourself as an adult. I know that might be asking too much, though."

"I don't need a live-in maid," Griffin snapped.

"You do, honey. But she's not going to live here," his mother said. "She's going to help you organize your office the way you want to and the way it needs to be done. She knows how to program, so she's going to update your website. She'll run your social media for you so you actually have an online presence."

"You know what social media is?" he asked, his brain going in a hundred different directions.

"I can tweet and Facebook like nobody's business, young man. Now let me finish!"

He lowered his head at his mother's tone. Fuck, it was like he was still a little kid.

"Anyway, she's going to help you run your life. Your brain is hurting right now, and sitting in your own filth and worrying about your deadline isn't helping. So we're stepping in and showing you that you can be an adult."

"And you can't back out of it," Miranda sighed. "No matter how much you want to."

"She's going to help you run your life because God knows you can't do it yourself," Maya added.

"And you can't fire her because *we're* the ones that hired her," Meghan added then frowned. "Though you'll be paying her since you make more money than us, but whatever."

Griffin pinched the bridge of his nose. He didn't

want a PA or anyone in his home when he needed to work. The thing was, he *wasn't* working. He *knew* he needed help, but that didn't mean he wanted to deal with it.

"Who did you hire?" he asked, his voice low. "Who do you think can work with me and take over my life? Because that's a lot of skills you're talking about. In fact, that sounds like it's more than one person's job."

"Well, you can't do it all even though you think you can," Maya said. "And you'll like her." He looked up at his sister to see the wide grin on her face. "In fact, I think you already *do* like her."

"Who?" he asked again, his fists clenching.

"Autumn, of course," Meghan said with a smile. "Who else would be able to handle you and your bad tempers other than *Fall*?"

"And you can't say no," his mother reminded him. "It's already taken care of. You're stuck with her, and you will treat her with respect. Got me, boy?"

Griffin closed his eyes and groaned. Well, fuck. "Autumn? You're kidding me, right? I thought she worked with Meghan?"

"She does," Meghan answered. "And she will work with you. And you'll be happy about it. Because if you mess with her and piss her off, she'll kick your ass. And then I'll kick your ass because she's my friend."

Griffin wanted to kick the girls out and stomp back to his room. There was no way this would work. Autumn would take one look at his place and run away. There was no way she'd want to stay and work with him. There was also no way he'd be able to deal with her so close to him while he was trying to figure out what the fuck to do with his book.

Maybe that was it. Maybe he'd let her see what she was in for and let her walk away. Because no matter what, Autumn couldn't be his personal assistant. No one could. He lived alone, worked alone, and breathed alone. It was the way he'd worked so far, and damn it, it was the way he would continue to work.

There wasn't another option.

Autumn wouldn't last long, and then she'd be out of his life forever.

And why the hell did that make his stomach hurt? For that reason and more, he knew he had to find a way out of this. Only he wasn't sure how he was going to do that with the women in his life staring at him the way they were. They wanted Autumn in his life, and the damned woman had said yes. And it looked like Griffin didn't have a choice at all.

Well, shit.

CHAPTER THREE

What the hell had she been thinking? Autumn didn't just react when it came to her life. She couldn't afford to. It might look like she went from job to job, place to place, without second thoughts or a care in her head, but she worked hard at that misconception. She didn't move without doing as much research as possible so she could make sure she wasn't followed. Or at least be as sure as she could. She also didn't take jobs randomly, despite the fact that she had held so many since high school her resume looked as if it had been patchworked from four different people rather than merely one. That was, of course, if she'd actually *had* a resume...

Yet when Meghan has approached her with the offhand comment of helping Griffin, she'd said yes.

Griffin's sister had wanted to help her brother but knew she couldn't do it all. While Autumn was happy Meghan wasn't trying to take everything on herself, she shouldn't have said yes to the other woman.

It made no sense.

Sure she could clean, cook, organize, program and pretty much do most of the things Meghan thought Griffin needed, but she shouldn't have said yes. The damned man had called her *Fall*.

Yeah, he'd rolled his eyes after he'd said it, so at least he hadn't been too serious. And to be honest, she'd laughed a little at the joke because it was *that* bad, but still. She shouldn't be getting closer to the Montgomerys. She should be severing ties so she could pack up and leave as soon as she could. She'd done her damndest over time to make sure no one truly knew who she was. That way, by the time she moved away, people would only remember a faint whisper of her presence. Unlike here, where she'd been given nicknames and worked with the whole family in one way or another.

The damn Montgomerys sure knew how to wrap a person up in their web of family, connection, and happiness.

It was enough to give a girl on the run an ulcer.

She didn't want to work for Griffin. The man was

too sexy for his own good. She had practically swallowed her tongue the last time she'd seen him, and now she'd be in his house. Daily. For hours. Alone. Just him and her. And the voices in his head that led to a book. She had to admit she was fascinated with his process since she didn't actually know anything about it. She'd always wanted to know how someone could write a book. She might have ideas and love reading, but she couldn't sit down in front of a computer or a notebook for hours at a time and try to build a story.

Autumn had read his books—though she hadn't told him that. The man was talented, and while she usually saved as much of her precious income as possible, she usually forked over the money for a hardback as soon as the book released.

But she wouldn't mention that to him either.

Not when she couldn't stop staring at those Montgomery blue eyes that looked so freaking sexy. The other Montgomerys may have similar eyes, but no one had ones as beautiful as Griffin's in her opinion.

And that was why she couldn't work for him.

She'd be cleaning up after him, organizing his life, getting in the way... There was no way she'd be able to do all of that and remain professional. Of course if she gave herself any credit at all, she would remember that she'd worked with sexy men all her life. She could just get over it. She hadn't had a serious relationship yet, and she wouldn't start now—not with the state of her life. So she wasn't about to fall for a man, especially not one who would dare to call her *Fall*.

The real reason that she couldn't work for him was that she was getting too close to the whole family. It would be harder to leave when the time came—and that was soon. They might miss her or want her forwarding address. She couldn't afford to have either occur.

But because she was an idiot, instead of packing up her belongings and heading out of town, she stood on Griffin's doorstep, his spare key in hand, and her throat as dry as a desert.

Because that made total sense.

She adjusted the strap of her cross-chest purse that she kept with her no matter the outfit she wore and lifted her hand to knock. She wouldn't use the key Marie Montgomery had given her yet. The older woman had mentioned the week prior when Autumn was hired that Griffin might not be the most...energetic when it came to the idea of a personal assistant—one more reason not to accept the position—and had given Autumn a key in case Griffin didn't answer the door. She'd also mentioned that his not answering the door could be for a number of reasons—he was working, sleeping, or otherwise occupied. Or he could just not *want* to answer the door and let her in.

Hence why most of the Montgomerys walked into each other's homes whenever they felt like it. It was as if they trusted one another to try and respect their idea of space and personal boundaries.

Such a strange concept.

The door opened with her hand in the air, hovering just off the door while she contemplated running back to her car and leaving Denver altogether. She blinked, her mouth going dry once again at the sight of him.

Griffin stood in the doorway, his hair disheveled as if he'd just woken up and hadn't bothered to run his hands through it in an attempt to tame it. He also had lines from his pillow on his face, and his eyes were only partially open—the early morning light much too harsh for him.

Her gaze traveled down from his face to his bare chest and she had to force herself to not lick her rapidly drying lips. He had a sprinkling of hair on his torso—no over-manscaping for him—and ink on his pec, sides, and part of his neck. His washboard abs looked like he spent hours at the gym, yet not crazy like some of the overly muscled men looked. The deep V at his hips pointed to a nice happy trail that ended at the top of the jeans he'd left unbuttoned. From the look of him, he'd hastily put on a pair of pants to get to the door, but hadn't bothered to button the fly...or put on underwear.

Was it getting hot out? She was pretty sure she could feel sweat roll down her back at the sight of him.

"You." His voice was gruff, unused.

She shot her gaze to his face as he ran his hand over his beard. "Me."

Oh, good. Articulate. Mature. Professional.

Was there a hole she could bury herself in for a bit? She didn't need a deep one or anything.

"I thought I heard someone on the porch," he mumbled. "I need coffee." He stood back then turned away, walking deeper into the house.

She blinked. Uh...what was that? Should she follow him? Was he not a morning person? Maybe he wasn't a people person. Why had she taken this job again? Oh, yeah, she was a glutton for Montgomery punishment apparently.

She took a hesitant step forward then paused. No, she couldn't be tentative. She needed to be forceful, commanding. She needed to make this man into a better author and a more organized individual, and being a timid kitten around him wouldn't work. She needed to raise her chin and walk in with a presence.

Autumn rolled her shoulders back and took another step into the room, only to freeze.

Dear. God.

The man cave had exploded, dying a fiery death of disorganization and clutter. Clothes were strewn over every piece of furniture he had. Dust covered the end tables and coffee table, though there wasn't any on his crazy-ass large flat-screen TV mounted on the wall. Of course that made sense, as he'd want to watch TV without dust interfering. From the cotton shirts on the cabinet under the TV, she figured he used those to wipe it down when the layer of dirt got to be too much.

Thankfully, she couldn't see any trash or crusty dishes beyond coffee cups lying around. So maybe it wasn't dirty...it was just messy. But still.

How did anyone live like this?

Oh, she forgot the books.

So. Many. Books.

Paperbacks, trade paperbacks, hardbacks. Stacks of papers that looked like they were an older manuscript clipped together. And was that...yes, that was an eReader pressed between the pages of a hardback as if it were a bookmark.

Dear. God.

The man obviously loved to read, but he didn't love putting his books back on the shelves. Of course, from the look of the shelves that lined the walls, she wasn't sure *where* he'd put the rest of his books. They were full to capacity and stuffed to the point she was afraid they would buckle if they hadn't been made of such sturdy wood. Knowing the rest of the Montgomerys, Storm or Decker had probably made them for Griffin.

And this was just the part of the house she could see.

She didn't even want to *think* about the bathroom.

The bathroom she would have to clean.

She shuddered.

"That bad?" Griffin asked, holding out a coffee cup. "I think I remember you having sugar and cream in your coffee at Taboo. I don't have fresh cream so you're stuck with the powered stuff. Sorry."

She took the cup that looked clean and full of fresh coffee from him. He raised a brow then took a deep drink from his mug after blowing on it.

"Ahh..." he whispered into his cup, looking down at his coffee like it was made from the gods, rather than a machine. "I don't have anything in this house most days, but I always have coffee. I used to have groceries delivered, but then I got stuck in my book and forgot to order again. But coffee? I have that on an automatic delivery." He quirked a grin at her, and she was pretty sure her womb clenched.

Seriously. Her womb.

How the hell was that even possible? And come to

think of it, that kind of clenching wasn't sexy in the least. This man was single-handedly burning her brain cells. Soon, she'd have a single brain cell left, singing a sad little tune about being lonely.

"I see," she said slowly. She took a sip of her coffee, praying he hadn't poisoned her or something then sighed. "Damn."

Griffin smiled full out. "I know, right? I live on this stuff. Best coffee in the world. I have a fancy maker in the kitchen that I grind beans for, but in my office, I have one of those one cup machines so I don't have to get up often."

Apparently, the best coffee in the world allowed Griffin to use his words. Of course, with the taste of manna on her tongue, she could probably formulate a sentence or two, as well. She didn't want to think about the cost of such coffee. But maybe she could hold the cup closer when he wasn't looking and cuddle it. On the other hand, that could be too much.

"So, you're here," Griffin said, rocking back on his heels.

She didn't forget he was shirtless and all sexy in front of her, but she refused to look below his chin. That wasn't easy since he was pretty damn tall, but he was now her boss. There were rules. Etiquette and the like.

Damned if she could remember it all right then, but she'd do her best to try.

"I'm here." She looked over his shoulder at the clock mounted on the wall. "I'm early, but I didn't know what schedule we would have. Your family hired me, but technically, I work for you so I figured we'd find a pace that works for us and move on from there."

"You're right. I didn't hire you. I'm not sure I even need you."

She held in what she really wanted to say after seeing his home and let out a breath. "You're behind on your deadline and your home is a wreck. I think you need me more than you know."

Griffin snorted. "And you think you can fix all that? Sorry, but I've been doing fine on my own all this time. I don't *need* you."

Ouch. She didn't know why that phrase hurt as much as it did, but she ignored it. Apparently, bonding over a love of coffee wasn't enough to make this day easier. Well, he'd just have to deal. Because she might have known this was a mistake, but she didn't back down when it came to doing what she had to.

She set her coffee cup on the dusty side table and raised a brow of her own. "Really? You're doing just fine on your own? Then why can't you order groceries like an adult? Why can't you dust your house? Or, you know, keep a cleaning service? I hear it's because you don't like other people having to depend on you for time and that nonsense. I think it's all because you think you can do it on your own, and you *want* to do it on your own, but can't. That's fine. You don't have to. You're successful enough that you can hire someone. And your family did it for you. So get over yourself and let me help. You want to focus on your book and actually write? Then do it. I'll take care of the rest. Because sitting in your own dust and dirty clothes without a proper meal isn't helping."

Griffin lifted a lip in a snarl but looked like he was holding himself back from yelling at her. Well, that was good. She hadn't meant to say all of that to him just then. She was usually a bit nicer when it came to other people's feelings, but there was something about Griffin that might not set her teeth on edge, but did something close enough to it that she didn't know how she'd react in any given situation. And that was freaking dangerous for a girl like her.

He ran his tongue over his teeth then slid his hand into the pocket of his jeans. And no, she didn't take a peek at what that hand would do for the bulge beneath his fly. Nope. Not her. She was professional.

Almost.

"What are you going to do for me? Hold my hand when I try to write?"

She rolled her eyes. "Oh, get over yourself, writer boy. I'm not going to look over your shoulder while you try to put words on paper because, hell, I don't know what I'm doing when it comes to writing. But I can help you with other things. First, your place is a mess. How you can breathe in here is beyond me. And I hope to God you bring your dates to their homes or a hotel or something because one look at this house and they'd run screaming."

She shut her mouth, her eyes widening. She so did not need to think of him with his dates. Now, she could only imagine him naked above his date—who happened to be her, of course—sliding in and out of her oh so slowly, his gaze on hers, never breaking contact. He'd flex his ass as he slowly tilted his hips up, fucking her with such a sweet seduction that she'd come achingly long over his cock before he filled her, groaning her name as he fell off the high cliff along with her.

Her cheeks burned, and Griffin tilted his head, studying her. "I don't bring my dates here. But I'd pay a whole hell of a lot to find out what just went through your mind just then, Fall."

That brought her out of her embarrassment. "Fall?

Really? Are you like twelve? I thought you were a writer. Can't you come up with something a bit more clever?"

"I could, but I like the look on your face when I say it. It's a mix of annoyance and laughter that I can't quite place. So you're stuck with that if you're not going to just go away."

"I'm not leaving."

"Fine. But I don't know what cleaning my house will do. I'm still not bringing dates here because this is my place. The one you're currently invading. And while I'm here, I need to work, yet I don't think you cleaning will help with that."

"It couldn't hurt." The word *invading* irked her, but she ignored it. He'd just have to get over himself.

"You'd think. But I fired the other cleaning services because they messed with my writing time."

"Put on headphones, then. Because I'm cleaning. And cooking because you can't survive on coffee, takeout, and the occasional meal at a family member's for long. You're in your thirties. You need to take care of yourself."

From the look of his body, good genes and working out helped, but the damn man needed vitamins, as well.

Enough thinking about his body.

"So you're going to cook, clean, and I take it shop?"

Griffin sucked in a breath. "And all of that should free me up so I can write?"

She wanted to scream at his attitude but stopped herself when she saw the look in his eye. The man was scared. Or at least something close to it. She knew he was behind on his deadline because the family had told her, but *why* was he behind? Could he not write at all? Because if that were the case, it would be a shame. She loved his worlds, the way he wrote, and everything about his books. And if she could help him at least a little bit, it would be worth the attitude.

"I don't see how it couldn't help. Plus I'm going to revamp your site." She frowned. "Wrong word. From what I can see, your site has a decent template. I can just update it and make it so your readers know what's coming next. Things like that. And I'm going to get your social media working because readers need to know who you are."

Griffin narrowed his eyes. "They don't. They just need my books. That's it."

She waved her hand at him. "You're a thriller writer, honey, you only think that. I'll help you and make sure I don't make it too personal, but have them think it's just personal enough." That last part was what she excelled at in real life. It couldn't be any harder to put it out on the Internet where there was a computer to shield her.

"I don't want them knowing everything about my life."

"And they won't. But they need to know you exist. At least a little. Also, I'm going to help you with a book bible or whatever else you need."

"Don't touch my books."

She held up her hands. "I will not ever touch your books while you're writing them. Nor will I harm your words. I just want to make things easier for you. It's why your family hired me. When I get the lay of the land, I'll know better what you need, but you need to know you're not alone in this. I'm going to help."

"And if I still don't want your help?"

"Suck it up, buttercup. I'm here to stay." *At least until I move away again.*

"Buttercup? Really, Fall?"

She flipped him off. Oh, perfect way to suck up to the boss. "Now, go to your office or whatever you need to do to get started for the day. I'm going to work on laundry. Or dusting. Or at least something so I can breathe in your house without feeling the need to shower."

His gaze raked her body, and her nipples pebbled into hard points, pressing into her bra and for damn well sure showing through her shirt.

"If you need to shower, Fall, go right ahead."

She snorted and flipped her hair over her shoulder. "Not until I clean it. I don't know where you've been." And with that, she pulled out a notepad and a pen, ready to take notes so she knew exactly what she needed to do and what supplies she'd need. Because this man's house was going to be a full-time responsibility, and the man himself was going to be even more.

She might be making a mistake, but at least she'd be good at it while she was making it. And if she kept telling herself that, she could try to ignore the way just the man's presence made her want to spread her legs and beckon him over.

Because that wasn't going to happen.

Ever.

CHAPTER FOUR

Griffin was in hell. A hot hell where the voices in his head didn't talk to him anymore and his cock was so hard he was afraid he'd rip through his jeans and embarrass himself.

Why had he told his mother that having Autumn over was an acceptable thing? Oh, yeah, he hadn't. He'd slightly given in but not fully. It wasn't like he could truly say no to his mom. Add in his three sisters, and he was screwed. He didn't like people in his space while he was working. Well, he didn't like people in his space on days he wasn't working either.

He had family over when he had to, and even let his cousins stay over since he had the most space for them. But that didn't mean he had to like it. Of course, none of this actually had to do with *why* he felt like he was in hell currently.

No, that privilege went to the woman currently humming in his living room.

Humming. Like she was actually happy about cleaning up after him. Damn it. He was an animal. A pig. A teenager who refused to clean his room because he was a fucking lazy screwup.

Of course, he hadn't truly thought that until he had a woman he didn't know but thought was fucking sexy as hell standing in his home and looking on in disgust. He wasn't filthy. There wasn't trash sitting around with bugs and shit, but still, he was cluttered. He knew that. He cleaned up when he could, and honestly, right now was the worst it had ever been.

And it was all because of this book.

This damn book that he couldn't write.

And, of course, he wasn't writing it like he should be right then because of *her*.

Fall.

Autumn.

Her.

He couldn't concentrate when she was so close. He could still scent the lotion on her skin; still feel the heat of her even though he hadn't touched her. He wanted to know if her skin was as soft as it looked, wanted to know if her lips would plump as he sucked on them, maybe even nibbled. He wanted to know the color of her nipples, if she had dimples on her lower back where her ass started to curve into that luscious shape.

He couldn't do that. He *shouldn't* do that. Thinking of her that way was disrespectful. She now *worked* for him. Autumn was off-limits, and yet his dick hadn't gotten the message. Instead, it strained against his fly, and he knew he'd end up with scars on the damn thing if he didn't shift around and do something about it at some point.

Of course he wasn't about to masturbate in his office—a man had limits. But he also couldn't go take care of it in the shower with Autumn here. Thankfully, he'd showered the night before so he at least didn't look too much like a dirty hoarder.

When Autumn had kicked him into his office, he'd pulled on a shirt from his clean stack of laundry and had gotten a lovely side-eye. He had a feeling his organization of dirty stacks versus clean stacks would be out the window with her around. He knew he should appreciate her help, but it still felt like a kick in the pants.

She'd pushed him out of the way three hours ago, and he'd written a page.

A page.

He wanted to weep with joy because that page was the biggest pile of shit he'd ever written. But he'd written.

One page in three hours. Only four hundred to go, and maybe he wouldn't have to slam his head into the wall. A light knock on his office door pulled him away from his empty second page, and he cleared his throat.

"Come in." He quickly looked around his office and winced. At least he didn't have dirty clothes in here. That had to count for something.

Autumn came in with a tray of food and a smile on her face. He quickly got up and took the heavy tray from her. He might be a mess, but he wasn't an asshole—most days. His mother had trained him well.

"I ordered in for lunch since you had that lovely delivery list attached to your fridge. I'll go shopping tomorrow once I figure out exactly what you need cleaning and food-wise. You had a whole cabinet of cleaning supplies, FYI." She raised a brow. "The layer of dust on said supplies was ironic to say the least."

He shrugged after he put the tray on the side table, trying not to meet her eyes. Yeah, he was embarrassed, but damn it, he needed to work. And sometimes things like showers, cleaning, and eating went out the window when deadlines called.

His stomach growled and he looked down at the food she'd brought. Burritos and a taco salad. Awesome.

"Thanks. What do I owe you for this?" He frowned. "How am I paying you exactly? Mom didn't mention it." He stacked a few books on the floor next to his desk so she'd have a place to eat if she, indeed, wanted to eat with him.

Autumn waved her hand. "Your mom took care of it. She gave me cash for food today actually, but I would have just paid for it and invoiced you. As for how I'll get paid, your sisters wrote up a contract that you should probably look at." She snorted. "They emailed it to you, but I figured you didn't check your email if you're that behind so I can print out what you need. As for payments, we can talk about that after we eat."

This time she wouldn't meet his gaze, and he tilted his head. Intriguing. It seemed Autumn had secrets. Secrets he wanted to uncover. Secrets he probably shouldn't uncover because he didn't *want* her to be intriguing.

Autumn took her taco salad and went to sit in his large leather chair, and he made sort of a strangled sound.

She froze, her very delectable ass hovering over the chair. "What the heck was that?"

He cleared his throat. "Not there. It's my thinking chair." And now he sounded like a fucking idiot. Maybe even like the crazy reclusive writer his family joked he was slowly becoming.

She stood straighter. "Ooookay, then. I can go sit in the living room and eat out there."

He closed his eyes and pinched the bridge of his nose. "No, you can sit at my desk or in one of the chairs at the table. I'm just really weird about that chair, okay? I promise I'm not a serial killer or anything. Or even crazy. I just…"

"You don't like people sitting in that chair. Got it." She shrugged, but he saw the laughter dance in her eyes. She sat in one of his spare chairs and his shoulders relaxed some. Yes, he was certifiable.

"Thanks," he mumbled. "And thanks for the food." He sat down in his desk chair—leaving the thinking chair empty—and dug into his food. Spice and cheese exploded on his tongue and he moaned.

"Good?" Autumn asked with a smile.

"Hell, yeah. I love this place." He took another bite big enough to make him look like a Neanderthal, but he didn't care.

"So, Griffin Montgomery, tell me about yourself." Autumn dug into her taco salad. He held back a grin. Like his sisters and Sierra, Autumn ate like she liked food, rather than nibbling at lettuce and calling it a meal. Good on her.

"What do you want to know?" he asked, trying to be civil. He still resented the fact that she was here, but he couldn't act like an asshole *all* the time. It got tiring.

"I don't know," she answered. "Tell me anything."

How about how he wanted to bend her over the desk and fuck her? No, probably not that. Damn it, he didn't like the sound of his thoughts right then. He was a fucking prick and he knew it.

"I'm a writer."

Autumn blinked, lowered her fork then did a slow clap. "Oh my God. That is...that is so *thrilling* to hear. I mean, you're a writer? Who knew?"

He lifted his hand to flip her off then remembered she wasn't family and ran his hand through his hair instead. Smooth.

"Wait. Did you just use the word thrilling on purpose?"

She rolled her eyes. "Nothing gets past you."

"Well, Fall, I'm a thriller writer. As you well know. Ever read me?" He smiled as he asked it and watched the way her eyes darted from his.

Intriguing. Again.

"I'm sure I have," she said vaguely.

He didn't know why that annoyed him, but it did.

So what if she hadn't read him, or if she had, didn't remember. It wasn't as if he didn't sell books.

No, he just couldn't write them.

God, he wanted her out of his house so he could think again. He hated that he'd put himself in this position.

"I'm the sixth kid in the Montgomerys," he blurted, wanting to keep his mind off the fact he hated his life right then.

"You're one of the babies, then." She licked sour cream off her fork, and he had to blink in order to think. Damn tongue of hers. She *worked* for him. Though maybe she worked for his mother if he thought about it, but damn it, he shouldn't be having dirty thoughts about Autumn. It wasn't fair to her, and it sure as hell wasn't fair to him.

"Alex and Miranda are younger, but yeah, I guess I am." He shrugged. They were all older now, so age didn't truly matter anymore when it came to how they interacted. Yeah, Miranda was still the darling baby, but she was married and happy. Alex had been one of the first married and now lived in rehab, trying to get his life together. Griffin...well, Griffin was just Griffin. And maybe that's why his brain couldn't work anymore.

And enough of that shit.

"I still don't know how you ended up here," he said, trying to break the rising tension in the room.

Her back stiffened. "What do you mean *here*?"

He frowned. "I mean working for me. What did you think I meant?"

She waved her hand. "Nothing. Meghan cornered me and I had a weak moment. I have the skills to help, and once I get the lay of the land, I'll let you know what I'm doing."

He raised a brow. "Shouldn't I tell you what *I* need?"

"Maybe. But if you could do that, you'd be doing it yourself, right?"

Okay, that was enough. "Fuck this. Just go home, okay? Thank you for cleaning and getting lunch, but I don't need help."

She rose slowly, methodically cleaning up after herself. "You're an idiot, Griffin, and you can't fire me. You can get over yourself and realize that you need help. I'm sorry for saying what I did. It was out of line. Of course you can't do it all, and you shouldn't. That's why I'm here."

He ran a hand over his face and turned away from her, needing to think. His eyes rested on the blank page on his monitor and, of course, instead of blaming himself for not being able to get past one page, he reacted like an idiot. He turned to her and put his hands on his hips.

"Go home, Autumn. I don't know you. I know you say you have these skills, but what do I really know, huh? You think you can just come in and take over my life? I don't think so. I'm not some kid who needs a babysitter. I'm a fucking man who has a job to do and can't do it with you lurking around."

Her cheeks pinked as he spoke, and he watched the rise and fall of her chest as she took deep breaths.

"You're an asshole."

"Yeah. I am. So you don't need to be around me."

"I'm done with this for today, but I'll be back."

"Don't bother." See? Asshole.

She flipped her red hair over her shoulder and glared. "You need all the help you can get, and the fact you can't see that just makes me sad. I'm going to help you because, damn it, I want you to finish your fucking book. So get over yourself and learn that you don't need to do it all on your own. That you *can't* do it all."

With that, she slammed the office door behind her. He counted to five, and then heard her slam the front door, too.

Well, he'd truly gone and pissed her off. But he couldn't work with her here. Of course, he ignored the fact that he'd written a whole page with her in the house—more than he'd written in a week. But that didn't count. He'd just delete that page anyway. He didn't know where his character was going, and he damn well sure didn't know where he was going.

Being royally fucked didn't even begin to cover the state of his life just then.

And it was all his fault. Not Autumn's. Not his family's. His.

And what was he going to do about it?

Not a damn thing it seemed.

Real fucking mature.

He looked at the clock on his phone and cursed. What the hell had he been thinking? Oh, that's right. He hadn't been. He quickly saved his one page on his computer in case something happened and stuffed his phone in his pocket. He pulled on shoes, got his wallet and keys, and left the house, locking up behind him. He stood on the porch, frowned, then unlocked his front door and took a step back inside.

Holy fuck.

He was a dead man.

An asshole.

An unworthy, ungrateful piece of shit.

He walked through the living room, his eyes wide.

Autumn had been in his home for only three hours and had worked miracles. His living room and dining room sparkled. Fucking sparkled. It smelled of lemons and lavender—not like dude and gym shorts. She'd dusted, vacuumed—how he hadn't heard that was beyond him—and cleaned up his clothes and spare glasses. She'd pushed all the books to the side by the bookshelves, and he figured she planned on going back to organize them. He winced. He'd have to help with that. It might not look like it, but he had a system—one he'd outgrown with the increase in books. He should have asked Decker or Storm to build him more shelves a year ago, but he kept putting it off.

He quickly shot off a text to Decker to ask for more shelves like he'd made him before then stuffed his phone in his pocket once more. The damn woman had cleaned up weeks' worth of mess in a few hours. It looked as if she were about to tackle his kitchen before she'd brought him lunch. And instead of saying thank you for any of that, he'd thrown a damn tantrum.

No wonder he was single and lonely.

He ran a hand through his hair and turned on his heel, walking through the now clean area back to his front door. Autumn had said she'd be back, and he'd say thank you. She'd cleaned up after him and done a better job than he could have ever tried for.

He had a full belly, a partially clean house, and one more page on his book than he had before. That was progress. And yet he'd yelled and pouted. What the fuck was wrong with him? So what if he had the hots for her? It wasn't her fault he wanted her and wasn't about to have her. And it wasn't her fault he was behind on his deadline, though he'd love to blame anyone but himself.

Griffin just hated anyone in his space, and the damn woman was more than just someone. She intrigued him, made him hard, and annoyed him all at once. Maybe he just needed to get laid. It had been long enough that he was afraid he'd forget how to do the deed once he was there.

His phone buzzed and he pulled it out again, grunting at the message from Decker.

About fucking time. Call me later and we'll get the details. At work now.

Griffin texted his best friend back saying okay and was about to put his phone away again when it started to ring. Apparently, he was popular today.

He answered when he saw Maya's name on the screen. "Hey."

"Hey, yourself. You coming in today for your appointment or are you going to keep scratching your balls for the rest of the day?"

He cursed. "Fuck. I forgot."

"Well, maybe if you put it on your calendar and set

up an alert, you wouldn't be such an idiot. Ask Autumn to make you a calendar for things like that. She'll keep you in line."

If she didn't quit first.

"I still can't believe you hired someone for me," he said, his voice dry.

"Well, you're not here, and I bet you weren't working if you answered your phone that quickly, so maybe you needed her. Now get your ass here so I can start your ink. Don't piss me off, Griffin."

She hung up on him, and he smiled. His sister was a mouthy, crabby woman most days, and he loved her all the more for it. And one day, if she ever saw the man she called her best friend for what he was worth, she'd end up a very happy woman. Of course, it wasn't his job to deal with that, so he'd step out of the way. For now.

He'd go get his ink, let the buzz of the needle and the pain of the tattoo wash away some of his anger, his self-pity. And when he got home, he'd write.

Like he'd been telling himself every fucking day for the past three months.

Though this time, he'd push Autumn from his thoughts and work on what he had to. And in the morning, he'd apologize for being an asshat and let her help.

Because he might resent her being there, but he'd written.

He'd *written*.

That had to mean something.

Eventually.

He hoped.

Because if it didn't? Well, he didn't want to think about that. He couldn't afford to. Ever.

CHAPTER FIVE

Autumn normally wouldn't hit a man. She wasn't prone to violence, but Griffin might end up the exception to the rule. The damn man frustrated her to no end, and it didn't help that he looked freaking hot all growly and stubborn. Add in a sheen of sweat and that broody glare, and she'd had to take deep breaths to keep under control.

Apparently, she was attracted to assholes.

Good to know.

It didn't help that she had to work for the damn man. First day on the job and she was already storming out, angry beyond measure, and genuinely upset that she'd caved at his demand for her to leave. She *knew* he hadn't wanted a true personal assistant working with him, but she hadn't known he'd be so resistant to the idea of help in any sort of way. He desperately needed it—if only to help him clear away the clutter in his mind. But he didn't want that. He wanted to do everything himself.

Yet he wasn't doing that, was he?

Freaking man.

With a sigh, she pushed open the doors to Montgomery Ink and let her shoulders relax—somewhat. Ink and friends would help. They always did.

Laughter, the buzzing of needles, and the deep growl of Austin's voice filled her ears, and she let out another sigh—this one happier. She could totally be at home in a tattoo shop. If only she knew how to tattoo. She could draw, but not like the immense talent of those in front of her.

"Autumn!" Callie, one the artists, came up to her, arms outstretched. Autumn leaned into them, inhaling Callie's sweet, floral scent. The woman bounced around like she had all the energy in the world, and looked kick ass while doing it. It helped that she was one of the younger people in the Montgomery world. It also helped that Callie was married to one damn fine man, who did his best to care for her every need.

No, that wasn't jealousy. Not even a little. Okay, maybe a little.

"It's good to see you, Callie." Autumn leaned back

and studied the woman's face. "There's something different about you."

Callie blushed, her eyes darting away. "I'm just happy."

Hmm...interesting. Well, it looked as if the other woman wanted to keep her secrets, and Autumn was fine with that. After all, she had enough secrets of her own to fill the entire shop and then some.

"You look it," Autumn said honestly.

"Thank fuck you're here," Maya shouted as she came up from the back room. The woman looked haggard as hell, but still damn sexy. If Autumn liked women that way, she was pretty sure Maya would be her type. Blunt, dark brown bangs framed her face and eyebrow ring perfectly. Bright red lips against the paleness of her skin made her look like a pinup star with a bit of an edge. Most of the ink on her body was done by her brother, Austin, the rest by herself. Seriously, the woman had talent. And an attitude. Hence why she was one of Autumn's closer friends—or however close Autumn let people be.

"Good to see you, too," Autumn said, her brow raised. "What's up?"

"Austin and his big oaf fingers fucked up the computer again," Maya snarled in her brother's direction. Austin, his attention on his client, used his free hand to flip his sister off.

There was a reason the Montgomerys were her favorites.

"Stop being mean," Callie said. "I can fix it."

Maya shook her head. "You have a client in five minutes. Or maybe you don't. I can't tell since I can't fix the fucking computer."

"I didn't fuck it up," Austin growled, his eyes still on the piece in front of him. "I pressed save. It didn't save. It's the computer's fault. If you hadn't fired the fucking receptionist who had actually managed to last two weeks, we wouldn't be in this damn situation."

Autumn pressed her lips together, trying to hold in her laughter. These two *always* spoke to each other like this within the confines of their co-owned shop. Of course, she was pretty sure they talked like this to each other everywhere else, as well. If she didn't know that either one of them would lay down their lives for the other, she'd have thought they had issues with each other.

"I fired the fucking receptionist because she kept trying hump your leg!"

Autumn gripped Callie's hand and refused to look at her. If *either* of them laughed just then...well, Autumn didn't want to think of the consequences.

"Like I'd let her close enough to hump my leg," Austin grumbled.

"She got pretty close once," Sloane added in, like the male he was. Damn fine male at that. All broad shoulders and thick thighs with a shaved head and a perpetual scowl. The man only grinned in truth for Hailey, though the café owner never noticed. Or maybe she did her best to *not* notice. Seriously, it was like a daytime drama in here sometimes, and Autumn loved it. If only she could work at Montgomery Ink and not for the big bastard author who refused to ask for help.

"Yeah, and I pushed her away and didn't make her cry like *someone* did."

"She deserved it!" Maya shouted.

Autumn took a deep breath and placed herself between the two siblings. Sure, Austin sat on his stool and hadn't moved forward, though he'd stopped tattooing once he turned his attention to his sister. The client just grinned, his full back piece looking like it had taken a few sessions. He had to be used to Austin and Maya by now. Maya had her hands on her hips, and her jaw looked as if it were ready to break, she'd clenched it so hard.

"Okay, folks, let me work on the computer and get you settled," Autumn said calmly. "I told you before that I would help with things like this."

Maya frowned then narrowed her eyes. "Wait. Aren't you supposed to be at Griffin's right now? I thought you were starting today?"

Autumn raised her chin. "Your brother's growl makes Austin sound like a puppy."

Austin barked out a laugh. "Fuck that kid sometimes. What did he do now?"

"He doesn't want an assistant."

"I could have told you that," Austin said, laughter dancing in his eyes. "But that doesn't mean he doesn't need one. He's just a bastard sometimes. Ignore him and do what you do best. Though I wasn't happy that the girls and Mom went behind his back to hire you, I think you're going to kick his ass in gear."

"Every Montgomery man needs a good kick in the ass sometimes," Maya said.

Austin raised a brow. "The women need the same thing, honey. Shall we talk about Jake?"

"He's just my friend!" Maya shouted. "How many times do I have to fucking say that?"

"And we're done," Autumn interjected. "Back to your corners. Both of you."

Maya grinned at Austin, but it looked a bit more feral than a smile. Austin just smirked, his lips barely visible in his beard.

"Do you think we could have one conversation

without cursing?" Callie asked, her eyes bright and innocent.

Maya snorted. "This from the woman who was just telling me how Morgan tied her to the bed and wouldn't let her come until she said how bad a girl she was."

Austin's shoulders shook, and Sloane chuckled as Callie, despite how red her face had gotten, raised her chin.

"Well, I *was* a bad girl, and I deserved to be punished. And I told you that in confidence, you whore. Maybe *you're* the bad girl and I should get Jake to punish *you*." She grinned, and Autumn had to move to the desk so she wouldn't fall down laughing.

"Next person who comments on Jake gets my foot up their ass."

"Did someone say Jake?" Griffin asked as he strolled into the shop. "You finally hit that, Maya darling?"

Maya growled while Autumn froze. What the hell was he doing here? He was supposed to be back at his home pretending to write and thinking about his asshole actions.

Maya launched herself at Griffin, her fists raised. Instead of ducking, he caught his sister and twirled her around the shop.

"I'm going to kill you," Maya said.

"I'm sure you'll try. But before you do that, you have to work on my next set of ink. My appointment, remember?"

Maya snarled. "I remember, but I'm surprised you did. In fact, how can you remember anything if you're kicking out your assistant before she can even start."

Autumn straightened her shoulders as Griffin looked up from his sister and met her gaze. He swallowed hard then clenched his jaw. The couple of days' worth of beard still looked mighty sexy on him. It wasn't as if she'd been out of his presence for long. How was it possible that he looked even *better* than before?

It was official. She'd gone crazy. Next stop: insane and drooling. And not drooling from how delicious the man looked. She would *not* be doing that. Ever.

"I didn't know you'd be here," Griffin said casually.

"You didn't ask."

"You didn't give me much time to ask, did you?"

Autumn opened her mouth to yell, then remembered where she was and who exactly was watching them act like six-year-olds fighting over a stolen toy.

"I wasn't aware you had an appointment here today," she said instead. With a few click of keys on the keyboard, she had the appointment book open and spotted Griffin's longstanding appointment with Maya.

"I had it down on a notepad in my office," Griffin said easily. "I'm not going to forget ink."

"No, you're just going to forget everything else." She winced. Damn it. This man was *still* her boss. She needed to remember that.

Maya snorted. "That's the truth. Ink before life. Right, baby bro?"

Griffin shook his head. "You're only one step up in the line, Maya. You're not that much older."

"Still counts." Maya frowned. "At least until I get to the point where I'm saying I'm still twenty-eight or something. Then you'll be older. Anyway, go sit in the chair and take off your shirt so we can work on finishing your shoulder piece. Don't flex too much though, darling brother of mine. The only people in this room with breasts are either related to you, married, or seem to hate your guts right now." She glanced at Autumn and winked.

Oh, good. This was going to end well. Now she had to be in the same room as a shirtless Griffin while the buzz of the needle filled her ears and made her even *more* turned on when it came to the bane of her existence Montgomery.

Autumn turned her attention back to the computer and did her best to make it a little more organized. Austin and Maya were totally methodical and ran one hell of a business that had a waiting list three years long for larger pieces and custom works of art. But the running joke of their lack of receptionist couldn't make things easy. Back when Callie had been Austin's apprentice and not a full-time artist, the younger woman was able to help out more, but now that word of Callie's own talent was spreading, she didn't have that kind of time. Autumn helped where she could and refused payment. Mostly because getting paid led to more paperwork, and the less paper trail, the better. So far, she hadn't had to file anything with Griffin, but she knew it was coming. She *hated* lying, but honestly, she had no idea what else to do. If things got sticky, she'd run like she always did.

Though this time, she knew running would hurt more than all the other times she'd done it.

Damn those Montgomerys.

She took a deep breath then turned toward Maya's station, just about swallowing her tongue as she did.

Griffin sat facing the back of the chair, his thick thighs spread so he could straddle the damn thing. He had his arms folded in front of his face, though he didn't lean on them. Instead, he turned his head to look over his shoulder at Maya as they talked about placement or whatever.

Autumn would *not* have an orgasm from the sight of him alone. She would *not*.

She pressed her thighs together and cursed the day Griffin Montgomery had been born.

She wasn't sure what Maya would be doing to Griffin's shoulder and back that day, and she wasn't sure she had the energy to stay there and watch. She had to keep whatever...this was to herself. There was no use lusting after a man she worked for—a man she'd eventually leave when it became too dangerous to stay.

Instead of lusting, she went back to the computer and cleaned up what she could. It didn't take that much time, and soon she found herself standing and rolling back on her heels, knowing she had to leave. She'd come to the shop to vent or at least calm down. But now that the source of her troubles was not only in the same damn room as her, but shirtless with just the right amount of chest hair to make her want to pet him until they were both begging, she knew she had to leave.

"Hey, Autumn, come over here right quick," Austin called out.

She closed her eyes and counted to five. "Sure thing."

She did her best not to look at Maya's station and act casual. She had a feeling she was failing miserably.

What the hell was wrong with her? She blamed hormones. Maybe she just needed to get laid and all of this would go away. Of course, with that thought, she could only imagine Griffin standing behind her, flipping her skirt over her hips as he bent her over his thinking chair and fucked her from behind.

Damn that Montgomery.

Damn them all.

"What's up?" See? That was normal.

Austin tilted his head, studying her face. "My client wasn't on-call but still had to go into work."

She frowned.

"Firefighter."

Her brows rose. "Is everything okay?"

Austin shook his head. "Not sure. Hopefully, his gear won't fuck up his ink, but fighting a fire is more important than anything I can do with his skin. Anyway, I have an hour now that's free. Sierra isn't across the street at her shop, or I'd just head there and see my wife. What do you think about sitting here and letting me work on that piece on your side?"

"What the hell? I thought I was the one who got her next?" Maya yelled from her station.

Autumn held back a grin. She loved the way these two always fought over family but not usually clients.

She warmed from the inside. Maybe she was getting closer...

Damn it. That wasn't good. She needed to leave town soon.

But before she did, she could at least get new ink.

"Sounds good to me," she said softly.

"Good. This'll repay you for helping us out so much since you won't take our money."

"But...but I can pay." She might not have endless funds, but she could pay for what she needed.

Austin narrowed his eyes. "Don't argue. Now sit down and roll up your shirt and tuck it under your bra. Let's get to work."

She opened her mouth to argue anyway, and the bearded, broody man in front of her raised a brow. Okay, then.

She did as she was told; aware that *someone* was staring at her. While one part of her might have wanted it to be heat coming from Griffin's gaze, she had a feeling attraction had nothing to do with it. When she ended up straddling the chair and facing Maya's station at a diagonal angle, she wanted to scowl.

Of course, she had to face Griffin and his sexy side and arms while she had her shirt tucked up. Why would the gods allow anything else?

Griffin met her gaze and quirked a grin. "Not what you expected your afternoon to look like, huh?"

She clenched her jaw. "Not exactly." She sucked in a breath as Austin touched her with the needle for the first time. It always hurt like hell at first, then went to a happy buzz that sent shocks of pleasure mixed with pain straight down to her toes. Griffin smiled at her then, that same look in his gaze.

She licked her lips, her heart racing.

His eyes dropped down to her mouth, his pupils dilating.

Oh, damn it. This was so not the place. So not the time. So not the guy.

Instead of letting anyone know what he did to her, she lowered her head and rested her forehead on her arms. Austin spoke to her every once in a while but seemed to know she needed time to herself—even in a busy tattoo shop.

Forty-five minutes passed in a blink as she focused on *not* focusing on Griffin. Soon she felt Austin wiping down her side for the last time and talking about aftercare.

"I think you'll be done with this one in one more session," Austin explained. "I could have finished the final shading today, but you were swelling a bit and I want to make sure it's perfect."

Autumn let Austin grip her hand to keep her steady as he led her to the long mirror. Her gaze traveled down the groupings of different bunches of flowers down her side—each flower representing a new place she'd been forced to occupy while never finding the space that was uniquely hers.

"It's perfect," she whispered. In fact, it looked finished. If she had to hightail it out of Denver right away, she wouldn't have to have anyone touch it up—not that she'd ever let anyone touch Montgomery ink. Only to a perfectionist's eye would there need to be extra shading or lines done.

"It's almost there," he said softly. "Now, don't forget to take care of yourself." He looked over at Maya and Griffin. "And kick his ass if you need to," he whispered, his beard tickling her ear.

She rolled her eyes then carefully slid her shirt over the plastic wrap he'd placed over her fresh ink. When she turned toward Maya's station, it was to see Griffin's eyes on her, his eyelids hooded as he raked his gaze down her. She wasn't sure if that look was for her alone, or a mix of the pain and pleasure that came with his own ink as Maya worked on his shoulders.

"I only saw a glimpse, but it looks fucking phenomenal," he said. He licked his lips. "See you tomorrow?" he asked, his voice hesitant.

She swallowed hard. She could do this. She could help him—then leave like she needed to. "Sounds good." With that, she said her goodbyes and left the shop, a cool breeze of Colorado mountain air chilling her red cheeks. She'd miss the scent of fresh and clean most of all...

By the time she drove home and pulled into her driveway, she was ready for food and a long shower. She couldn't soak in the tub thanks to her new ink, and she never liked to drink until her tattoo had healed a bit more since it thinned her blood.

When she stepped out of her car, her ever-present bag in her hand, she froze, the hair on the back of her neck rising. She swallowed hard then did her best to look casual as she searched her surroundings. Autumn might not have seen anyone, but it damn sure felt like someone was watching her.

She knew what that felt like.

Had felt it countless times before.

She quickly made her way into her home, her keys and pepper spray in her hands in case someone came at her. As soon as she closed the door, she set the deadbolt, hurried to the kitchen, grabbed the big butcher knife she knew damn well how to use, and searched the rest of her small house.

Alone.

She was safe.

At least for the moment.

But she knew her time in Denver was ending. She'd been here too long already...long enough that she'd formed attachments she never intended to keep.

Autumn would finish her promise to help with Griffin to the Montgomerys and herself and then she'd leave.

It would be safer for everyone. Because if she stayed, she'd be responsible for the carnage.

She always was.

CHAPTER SIX

"You're looking more energetic," Griffin said with a small smile as his dad engulfed him in a big hug. The man may not be as large as he once was, the hugs not as tight as they'd once been, but there was no denying that Harry Montgomery was a force to be reckoned with. Griffin had come over for an afternoon meal, and honestly, just to see his folks.

"I'm feeling like it," his dad said softly. "You here for a reason, or to check up on me?" He grinned and leaned back. "It's your turn, isn't it?"

Griffin rolled his eyes. Busted. Whatever. His siblings wanted nothing but the best for their parents, and things had been a shitty rollercoaster for the past few years. Between Dad's cancer diagnosis and subsequent treatments, Austin's drama with his kids and

Sierra, Decker and Miranda's rocky courtship and almost ruined wedding courtesy of Alex, and all the hell that Meghan had been through before she'd finally been able to settle down with Luc, Griffin worried.

Griffin worried about a lot of things. It was just something he did.

"We kids can't get anything by you. It's my turn, but I like coming here anyway."

"Because your mom feeds you, most likely."

Griffin shrugged, his grin unrepentant. "Well, that's a plus in the column for sure."

Marie came into the living room, a tray of drinks and an antipasto plate in her hands. Griffin quickly went to her and took the platter.

"You should have told me to get my ass in there to help," he admonished and set the tray down on the coffee table.

"I'm not feeble," she said then kissed his cheek as he handed her a drink. "But I like your help anyway."

Griffin bent and rested his forehead on hers as he'd done countless times before. He still remembered when she'd been the one to bend. Time flew, he knew, but damn, he didn't want it to go too fast; not when his dad wasn't out of the woods yet.

He sucked in a shaky breath—the emotions too

much—and stood. "All you have to do is ask. Anytime. Okay?"

Marie met his eyes and nodded. "Okay, Griffin darling."

Griffin settled into one of the couches after his parents did the same on the other, and drank and ate while they talked of their day-to-day issues and accomplishments. He liked days like this; liked it when he could just sit and listen to the two people who had raised him, had loved him with every ounce of their being. Life wasn't perfect—far from it—but sometimes he could forget his worries and just *listen*.

Of course, he couldn't ignore the drawn look on his mother's face. He knew she wasn't sleeping as well as she once had. She couldn't. Not with the love of her life in pain next to her. But things were looking up. At least that's what they told him. He had to pray they wouldn't cushion the blow if things went to hell. He was stronger than that. At least, he hoped he was.

"Have you heard anything from Alex?" Griffin asked finally, his hands around his glass. The condensation slid over his fingers, and he tightened his grip. He remembered the last time he'd seen his brother, the mad edge to Alex's eyes. He could still hear the sound of glass breaking as Alex screamed and raged. He'd ended Miranda and Decker's wedding early, his personal demons too much for any one person to bear. Only Griffin didn't know what had driven Alex to drink. No one did.

Harry let out a breath. "Yes, he finally let us talk to him over the phone."

Griffin carefully set his glass down and met his father's eyes. "And?"

"And he's staying in rehab, at least for the time being," his dad said softly. "I think he's finding the help he needs. Finally."

Griffin closed his eyes and let out a breath. His baby brother hurt, and yet there was nothing Griffin could do for him. Once Alex got out, he hoped there was a way he could help, but he wasn't sure.

"One step at a time, darling," Marie whispered. She cleared her throat, her voice louder when she added, "He'll come home when he needs to. And, hopefully, he'll let us visit him. He might think he's alone—at least that's what I got from that phone call—but we're Montgomerys. We don't leave each other behind, no matter how hard we try to push each other away."

Griffin smiled despite himself. Yeah, that sounded about right. He took another sip of his lemonade and nodded. "He can't get rid of us that easily."

"Damn straight," his father agreed.

After they'd finished their meal and said their goodbyes, Griffin headed back home, his stomach full and his mind a bit fuller. He knew he had to work since he hadn't written a word that morning and had spent his afternoon with his parents. But he *always* had to work. The resentment that came with that thought didn't make him feel any better.

When he pulled into his driveway, he didn't see the growingly familiar car that belonged to Autumn. He wasn't sure why he'd expected her to be there since he hadn't been home, but it was hard to ignore the pang of disappointment when he realized that she wasn't there.

It had been four days since he'd seen her at the tattoo shop. Four days of them working together in his home in silence. She cleaned, shopped, and kept him fed.

She'd yet to venture into his office to actually help with his work.

He had a feeling she would have done it sooner if he hadn't been such an asshole. Only it was fucking hard to *not* be an asshole sometimes. He rested his forehead against the steering wheel and let out a curse. He needed help.

He *knew* that.

It didn't mean he had to be goddamn happy about it.

With another deep breath, he got out of his car and

made his way to the front door. As soon as he opened it, he knew he'd been wrong. The scent of soup and freshly baked bread assaulted his scenes, and his previously full stomach growled. Autumn's light floral scent mixed with the hearty smell of food and his cock hardened.

Down boy.

It was weird that she would be there when he wasn't. He knew she had a key thanks to his ever-annoying and loving sisters, but he wasn't sure she'd actually use it. He also hadn't left a note saying where he would be since she hadn't been there when he'd left earlier. It wasn't as if he should have thought about it, really. She didn't *live* with him.

She worked for him.

Or at least tried to.

Autumn bounced into the living room and froze when she saw him. She had a basket of laundry under one arm and her phone in the other.

"Oh, you're home."

He closed the door behind him without looking, his gaze on her instead. She wore some kind of long dress today that hugged her curves without making her look like she'd tried for that effect. In fact, it looked as if she'd gone for comfort instead. He wasn't sure that she could ever hide her curves, the sexiness of her presence. Her breasts here high, larger than his palms, and damn it, he wanted to hold them, squeeze them, learn the feel and shape of her nipples...find out the color and taste.

But he wouldn't do that, of course.

He was a professional—even if he didn't always act like it.

He pulled his gaze from her breasts and caught the blush of her cheeks. Fuck. He wasn't handling this well. Instead of apologizing like he should, considering that would just make it even more awkward with the two of them standing there, he cleared his throat.

"I didn't see your car."

She nodded, her eyes trailing down his body. When she stopped at his groin area, he did all in his power not to adjust himself. He knew his dick pressed against his zipper, could feel it even, but he didn't want her to *know* he saw her staring.

Damn it.

"My car wouldn't start." A shadow passed over her face and he wondered what that was about. He always wondered about her expressions, wondered about *her*. "Meghan dropped me off. She said she'd pick me up or send Luc if you can't take me home." She winced. "Sorry for being a pain."

He shook his head. "Not your fault your car won't start. I'll take you home when you're ready." He put his hands in his pockets; aware he'd just forced her gaze to his dick again. "Just let me know. And do you need someone to check out your car? Or at least get you to the shop?"

She shook her head. "I'll take care of it. I just couldn't this morning." She paused. "But thank you."

"Okay then."

"Okay."

They stared at each other for at least a minute in awkward silence. He had no idea what to say next, what to do. He was a goddamn adult, and yet he couldn't voice his thoughts. He should at least move away and sit down at his computer or something. That had to be better than staring at her like a lustsick fool.

"I was just finishing laundry," Autumn finally said.

"I can see that." He pulled his hand out of his pocket and gestured toward the basket. "Uh, can I help?"

She blinked at him. "No, I've got it." She smiled wryly then. "Of course, if you had done your laundry to begin with, we wouldn't be in this situation, and I might not have a job."

He snorted, thankful she'd broken the ever-increasing tension. "Got it. Well...I guess I'll go to my office."

She smiled then, and he had to swallow hard at the beauty of it. He had no idea where that thought had come from, and he wasn't exactly comfortable with it.

"Sounds like a plan. I know you ate at your folks' house—that's what Meghan said at least—but if you're hungry, I put beef and barley soup in the Crock-Pot, and since you had a bread maker, I made a loaf of sourdough."

Again his mouth watered. "I have a bread maker?"

Autumn rolled her eyes. "Yes, you do. I had to clean it out since it wasn't in the box, but it still had the plastic and cardboard inside the base unit."

"Oh. That's cool. I'm stuffed, but that smells damn good, so maybe in a couple hours."

She smiled again, and he had to blink. "That's what I figured. So, yeah, you go into your office and write. I'll finish laundry. Once I'm done, though, do you think I can venture into your writing cave and work on your book bible?"

He frowned. "I already have a book bible."

She nodded. "That's what your editor said."

His brows rose. "You talked to my editor?"

She nodded again, this time her gaze lowered. "Yeah, she, uh, emailed me today. She was talking to Maya, and Maya mentioned me."

Griffin closed his eyes. Damn his sisters. He knew his editor wouldn't say anything about deadlines or anything confidential, but her being friends with Maya wasn't his favorite thing in the world.

"Okay, I guess. But if she said I already have a book bible, why are you going to work on it?"

She finally set down the laundry basket, and he could have kicked himself for not helping her as he'd helped his mother with the tray earlier. Autumn just put him off balance, and he wasn't sure how to work with that.

She let out a breath and stared at him. "I read you, Griffin. Did I tell you that before?"

He wasn't sure, but he liked the fact that she read him. It also left him a bit bare at the thought. "I don't remember."

She waved a hand. "It's no matter. But I read you. I actually like your books, Griffin."

He filled with pride, but he still didn't say anything.

"And as someone who enjoys your work, I want to make sure you can focus. That's why I'm here. So I'm going to take your bible and see what I can do with it. You shouldn't have to do everything. You should be able to look at your book bible and glean what you need from it and just continue on. I want you to be able to know that everything you need will be in there and that it will be organized so you don't have to worry. Do you have every single side character ever in your books? Do you have the color of a random dress from page seventy that might be important in the next book? Because that's what I can help with. If you can just focus, maybe that would help."

He knew what was helping, even if he was too tired and too stubborn to admit it.

Her.

Autumn.

Her presence alone was helping him write and it killed him. He'd written more in the past few days with just her near him than he had in the past two months. He didn't know if it was because she'd cleaned and cooked, or if it was for a far deeper reason that he'd rather not think about now, if ever.

And if she could take part of the admin work he'd been ignoring for far too long away from him, then maybe that would help, too. He loved his fans, his readers. He knew they were the reason he was able to do something he loved. The fact he didn't love it right then didn't mean he didn't love it at all. It was a love/hate relationship that made his writer brain usually yearn for more.

Only this time it was *Autumn* that made him yearn for more.

And that was damn dangerous.

"Griffin?"

He shook his head, trying to clear his thoughts. "I'll show you what I have when you come into my office.

I've been doing this for a few years now, so I know it might not look like I know what I'm doing, but I'm not that bad off."

She sighed. "I know you aren't bad off. I've read your work, remember? I hear you typing away in your office so I know you can work hard. You're letting me help bit by bit so I'm going to keep pushing until neither one of us can let me push anymore."

He nodded then tilted his chin towards the kitchen. "I'm going to go get a drink. Just walk into the office when you're ready to work."

He moved past her, careful not to brush against her as he did. As soon as he stepped into the kitchen, the mouthwatering scent of beef and barley made his body want to fall to the floor at Autumn's feet and beg for more. More of what...well... again, he wasn't going to think about that. But damn it, he hated himself just a bit more for it all. He had groceries in his home, food in his Crock-Pot, and found out he had a fucking bread maker because of the woman in the living room. He obviously *couldn't* take care of himself like an adult. He was a goddamn idiot—selfish and lazy.

"Why are you scowling? Did I not get you what you needed to make your drink?"

He cursed under his breath and lifted his head so he could see Autumn fully. She had her hands empty but was wringing them in front of her. He'd never seen her do that before, look so uncertain. And he was the one doing that to her. This strong, fucking amazing woman and he'd made her wring her hands.

"I'm just pissed off that my house is so fucking clean and filled with food because you're the one doing it. Not me. Like I'm a lazy asshole." He didn't know why he let the words come out of his mouth, and from the wide eyes on her face and open mouth, he had a feeling Autumn felt the same way.

"You're not a lazy asshole. All of what you said is what I'm here for. So you can think about other things. Damn, Griffin, you've earned that right."

He snorted. "Earned? Are you fucking kidding me? I just put words on paper. How is that earning."

She waved her hands in front of him. "Oh, shut up. You do more than you think. You can't quantify the way someone feels when they read a book, when they see an aspect of themselves in a character. Or even an aspect they want to be. I see what you do, I see how you struggle to make sure the book is *yours*, even though the reader thinks of it as theirs, as well. It's not just words, Griffin. It's a story, an idea. It's a life. You do so much more than you think you do."

He tilted his head, studying the way her cheeks had pinked with the passion of her speech, the way her breasts rose and fell as she took deep breaths. He loved the fire in her eyes, the way she *knew* things about him—the way he worked, the way he thought, even if he hadn't known he felt that way at all. Her pupils were wide, dark, and when she licked her lips, he was gone for her. He could tell she wanted him just as badly, and yet they'd pulled away over and over again, ignoring what was right in front of them because it was the smart thing to do.

But despite his accomplishments, Griffin knew he wasn't a smart man.

Not in the slightest.

He wanted her—body, mind, and maybe even her soul. But right then, he wanted *her*.

"The hell with it, Fall," he growled. He prowled the two steps between them, wrapped one hand around the back of her neck, his fingers tangling in her hair, and crushed his lips to hers. She gasped into his mouth before her arms went around his back, her nails digging into his skin beneath the cotton of his shirt. His free hand traveled up her side, trailing fingers up her arm, and then grasped her cheek, angling her face so he could deepen the kiss. Their tongues clashed, pushing against one another as they fought for control. He might have her in his arms, may have positioned her for what he desired, but she was the one who controlled him, who raked her nails along his shirt and skin, pushing him to go deeper, to kiss her until they couldn't breathe, couldn't think without wanting *more*.

This was Autumn.

The woman he wanted.

The woman he craved.

The woman who fucking *worked* for him.

At that thought, he wrenched his body away, his chest heaving. He took a step back, slid a hand through his hair, and let out a shaky breath. "Fuck."

"I...Griffin..."

He held up a hand, noticed it shaking, and lowered it. "I'm sorry. So fucking sorry. Forget that happened. It was just a momentary lapse."

She tilted her head but didn't look hurt. Thank fuck. "Okay. I need to go home." She groaned. "But I need you to drive me still." She closed her eyes and groaned. "You're right. We're forgetting that happened, but..."

He cursed again. "Let me grab my keys. You get that bag I never see you without and let's roll." He met her gaze. "I'm sorry."

She narrowed her eyes. "Say you're sorry again and I'll start to feel bad."

He gave one quick nod. "Got it."

She quickly got her bag, and he grabbed his keys.

Soon they were on the way to her place, an awkward as hell silence filling the car. He'd fucking kissed her.

No, that wasn't right. It hadn't just been a kiss. He had devoured her, a soul-clenching taking of lips and breath and heat. And he couldn't do it again. Not if he wanted to stay sane. He didn't know anything about her, and he knew she kept secrets, but he still wanted her. And that was more dangerous than anything else he could think of right then.

His hands clenched the steering wheel. "Autumn…"

"Don't, Griffin. I'll make sure I can get someone to drop me off at your place tomorrow for work. Hopefully, my car can get into the shop tomorrow, as well. We'll just work on your book bible, and then I'll get to work on your site. As you said, nothing happened."

He opened his mouth to say that he was sorry again, to say that he'd fucked up. And, yet, he didn't know what he truly wanted to say. Instead of being able to speak, he heard her scream and turned to his left.

Bright lights filled his vision, and the sound of crunching metal and Autumn's screams were the last things he heard before a fiery pain slammed into his body. He tried to hold out an arm, tried to somehow protect the woman next to him, but he couldn't.

Darkness engulfed him, pulling him under into a sweet splendor of agony and hell.

CHAPTER SEVEN

Autumn hadn't wanted to die, hadn't wanted to spend her last breath on a scream for a man she hardly knew but felt as if she'd known all her life. And she hadn't. Instead, she found herself in a hospital waiting room, bandaged and bruised and surrounded by countless Montgomerys. She also found herself unable to speak, afraid that as soon as she did, she'd break.

She hadn't let a single tear fall, but as soon as she spoke, she was afraid she'd let them *all* fall.

The others had only looked at her once, nodded, then sat next to or near her, waiting her out.

They might have to wait a bit longer because she sure as hell didn't know what she would say to them. How could she comfort them? Tell them their son, brother, and friend would be okay when she wasn't sure what had happened?

The car had come out of nowhere. It'd run a stop sign and slammed into the driver's side door. The police had mentioned drunk driving, and since she knew for a fact Griffin hadn't been drinking, it had to be the other driver. Her brain had only been focused on Griffin and the blood that had coated her clothes. She knew that it didn't all belong to her, and she didn't even know if the other driver was alive. The Montgomerys would be able to talk to the police and doctors for those details. She was useless until she could gather what little courage she had and figure out what the hell she was going to do.

Again she found herself in the presence of authority figures where she would either have to lie about her name and facts or tell them the truth. Despite what she felt sometimes, she wasn't actually on the run from the cops, so in the quiet she would be able to tell them her name if they required it. Everything was just so...*sticky*.

For the countless time that evening, she pushed her thoughts from her mind about the fear of what could happen if she said too much and focused on what mattered.

Griffin.

He hadn't been conscious when the EMTs had

pulled them out of the wreckage of what had once been Griffin's car. They'd said it was a miracle that Autumn hadn't broken a bone or received a concussion of her own. In fact, except for a few small cuts here and there and her body feeling like a giant bruise, she hadn't been hurt at all.

She should have been grateful; instead, she could only think of Griffin.

Jake slid into the empty seat Luc had just vacated and took her hand between his. She looked down at his large hands, noticed the specks of clay in the creases and under his nails, and focused on that rather than the lack of news on Griffin.

"I think you've figured this out already, but when you're ready to talk, we're here."

She looked over at the very handsome man with bright green eyes, who called Maya his best friend.

"Thank you," she whispered, her voice hoarse.

"Here." Autumn looked up as Maya held out a paper cup filled with water. The other woman's eyes were narrowed, her jaw set, but she didn't look angry. No, Maya looked worried as hell and was doing her best to try to mask it. It wasn't working in the slightest.

"Thank you," Autumn whispered again, taking the cup from Maya. She gulped half of it down quickly, letting the room temperature water soothe her aching throat.

"We've been in waiting rooms like this way too many fucking times," Austin growled from his chair across the room.

Autumn pressed her lips together and nodded as the others agreed. The rest of them started speaking of the earlier times they'd been there for the other Montgomery siblings, and Autumn had to take deep breaths to hold back her tears. Seeing them together like this just reminded her how *alone* she truly was.

She had no one.

It was her fault, of course. She'd been the one to leave that place, but it had been better than staying. She might miss her parents and her brother more than anything in the world, but they hadn't believed her. They hadn't stood by her when she'd needed them most. And because of that, she hadn't been able to lean on them when it truly mattered. Of course, now that she looked back at the young woman she'd been when she'd left, at the fear that had coated her veins, she could see that maybe they *did* believe but had chosen to ignore it because of their *own* fears.

It hadn't mattered, though. She'd left to protect them as well as herself. It wasn't safe for her to be with them. She looked around at the Montgomerys and knew she'd have to leave soon. It wasn't safe for them either.

It was never safe.

The doors to the waiting room opened and a nurse wheeled Griffin inside. Autumn stood, her empty cup falling to the floor. Jake squeezed her hand once then left her to wrap his arm around Maya's shoulders—whether he was merely holding her or holding her back, she didn't know. Nor did she care right then.

She only cared about Griffin.

Dangerous.

They'd put him in a pair of scrubs—much like the ones she now wore since her clothes had been covered with debris and blood. He leaned against the back of the wheelchair, his body cut and bruised like hers, but his eyes looked alert. His gaze searched the room as his family came up to him, but he didn't rest on a single person—until he reached her. As soon as their eyes met, his shoulders relaxed and his jaw loosened.

Autumn blinked, unable to voice her worries, her relief that he was okay. She pulled her gaze from him, unsure of what to do under the scrutiny. Her gaze landed on his right hand and she staggered back into Storm's solid chest. The cast on Griffin's hand made her want to retch, her body close to shaking. Her skin went clammy and her mouth dried.

His hand.

His work. His life. Oh, God.

Griffin.

She met his gaze again and she saw the pain in them this time, the pain that had nothing to do with agony, but with *knowing*.

"Are you okay?" he asked.

The room went silent.

She nodded, still unable to speak fully other than the few whispers she'd managed before.

His throat worked as he swallowed again before turning to look at his parents. "I'm okay."

"Oh God, Griffin," Marie cupped her son's cheeks gently. "What happened?"

Griffin leaned into his mother's hold as he spoke about the driver coming at them. Autumn wanted to leave. She felt like a voyeur, someone who shouldn't be there in the presence of such a tight-knit family. If she hadn't needed a ride, if she hadn't reacted as she had to Griffin's kiss, he wouldn't be here—hurt and broken. His livelihood wouldn't be in jeopardy because she was a selfish liar who didn't deserve the looks of comfort and concern she was getting. She turned to leave, but Storm put his hands on her shoulders. She let out a slight moan, and Griffin turned to her again, his eyes narrowing where Storm touched her.

"Shit," Storm whispered. He moved his hands away slowly. "Sorry, honey. I forgot the seatbelt got you."

"You should be sitting down," Griffin said, his voice low.

"I'm fine, Griffin," she said, her voice a bit louder than before.

"You're coming home with us," Austin said after a few moments of silence.

"No, you have the kids at home, he can come home with me," Wes said.

Soon, every single Montgomery offered—or rather announced—that Griffin would be staying with them. The show of love and compassion nearly brought her to her knees.

Griffin shook his head then winced. Autumn had taken an involuntary step toward him before she stopped herself.

"I just want to go home," he said finally.

"You need someone to wake you up every so often," Meghan said softly. "You can't be alone tonight."

Autumn's mouth opened before she even realized she was ready to offer. "I'll take care of him."

The Montgomerys turned as one toward her. Talk about intimidating.

Griffin's mouth quirked, and she saw the relief in his eyes. He didn't want everyone around him, seeing him like this. She didn't know what it meant that he seemed to be okay with her there, but she'd take it. It was the least she could do.

"I'm at his house most of the time anyway," she continued. "I don't have the same responsibilities like you when it comes to kids, health issues, or work."

Storm put his hand on the small of her back, and she saw Griffin's eyes narrow once more. "Sounds like a plan. I'll drive you, though, since I know you don't have cars here."

She could have hit herself. Damn it. Her car wasn't working—which scared the hell out of her since she needed it for escape, and Griffin's car was a loss.

"We'll get someone to check out your car, Autumn. That way you have a mode of transportation," Wes added.

"And I'll drop by in the morning to help or get you home if you need to pick things up," Storm added. "That is if you plan to stay the night. Do you?"

She blushed for some reason, though she'd been the one to offer to stay the night anyway. "I'll sleep on the couch."

Griffin growled.

Growled.

Maybe his pain meds were making him act more

possessive than usual. Or maybe *she* was the one who needed a nap.

"I'm fine," she said.

"You'll need rest, as well," Miranda said softly.

"Then I'll set an alarm. It will be okay."

Griffin glared. "Not the couch."

She blushed again before she remembered the size of his home. "I can stay in the guest room. Okay?"

"Fine."

She let out a breath, then let the rest of the Montgomerys ask the questions they needed to and say their goodbyes. Each one hugged her gently before helping them get to Storm's car. She sat in the back with Griffin in silence; aware that he kept staring at her as if he were trying to figure out what to say. It wasn't as if she knew what to say either.

Storm helped her get Griffin into his bedroom and snorted when the man noticed how clean the place was. At least she'd done a good job there. Storm left them with a dip of his head and locked the door behind him, leaving Griffin in his bed and Autumn wringing her hands beside him.

"I'm glad you're not hurt," Griffin whispered.

Tears filled her eyes, but she refused to let one fall. She needed to leave him alone before he saw her cry.

He reached up with his left hand and touched her cheek. "Autumn..."

She leaned forward and kissed his temple. "Goodnight, Griffin. I'll wake you soon."

"Autumn..." he repeated.

She pulled away, the lack of his touch like a cold burn. "Goodnight."

She turned on her heel as the first tear fell, knowing Griffin had seen anyway. He was hurt because of her, in pain because of her. And she shouldn't have been surprised.

Everyone always got hurt when they got too close.

Griffin looked down at his hands and frowned. One held only a scrape or two. The other was fully encased in a cast. The doctors had told him if he hadn't had his arm out over Autumn's body the way he had, he may not have broken it. As it was, he didn't need surgery, but it had been damn close.

His hand hadn't saved Autumn's life, but in that instant, he'd *needed* to somehow protect the woman sitting in his passenger seat.

It had been idiotic, but he wasn't sure he'd have done it differently if he had the chance to do it again.

Of course now he was royally fucked when it came to his deadline. His editor was sympathetic and had said she would extend it since they still had time. In fact, since he was usually so early with his manuscripts, he could theoretically make his original release date.

He just had to *write*.

How he could do that one-handed, he wasn't exactly sure.

He'd been awake off and on all night since Autumn kept coming into his room with her gentle caresses and soft words. She wanted to make sure his minor concussion wasn't worse than it had been, but it was a new form of agony to have her so close when he was in bed and not able to do anything about it. He cursed at himself. Damn it. He didn't have any right to want her. Kissing her had put him in this position in the first place.

He would not be kissing her again.

And if he kept telling himself that lie, then one day he might believe it.

"Griffin?" Autumn came into his bedroom with a tray in her hands. "I know you've been on the phone off and on all morning, but I made you breakfast."

He studied her face, the dark circles under her eyes, and wanted to bring her close, tell her everything was okay. But he knew that wasn't quite true. He didn't know what the hell was going on between them, nor did he know what he was going to do with his damn book. But on top of that, he knew she held secrets he wasn't sure she would ever share.

Griffin cleared his throat. "You didn't have to make me breakfast."

She set the tray down on the table next to the bed and put her hands on her hips. "Yes, I did. It's part of the job."

He didn't know why that statement hurt when it shouldn't have in the slightest.

Autumn let out a breath. "Plus, I wanted to. You shouldn't have to move a lot since your brain probably still isn't happy yet."

He raised a brow. "Thanks," he said dryly.

She rolled her eyes. "Oh, shut up. I was...well...I have no idea what I meant by that actually. Anyway, I have breakfast for you. And I'm sure your family will either be here soon en masse, or one at a time according to a prearranged schedule. So, after you eat, we'll get you showered and dressed and then we can figure out what we're going to do about your writing."

He licked his lips at the thought of her in the shower with him; his hands roaming over her body as he made sure every single inch of her was squeaky clean.

"Get your mind out of the gutter, writer boy. Your hand is broken, not your leg. You don't need me in the shower with you."

He met her gaze. "There might be a need..."

"Griffin."

He closed his eyes. "Sorry. I know we said we wouldn't talk about what happened in the kitchen, but—"

"And that would be talking about it," she interrupted.

"We should really talk about it sometime." Who was this guy? Hell, he never talked about relationships. Ever since Lauren, he shied away from talking about feelings and shit unless it was in a book.

At the thought of Lauren, he paused. What the fuck was wrong with him? He never thought her name anymore. He tried damn hard not to think about her at all. Maybe he'd hit his head harder than he thought. Or maybe it was all because of the woman in front of him.

"Or, we can go about our business." Her gaze landed on his bare chest and froze. When she licked her lips, he had to adjust his boxers. Pink laced her cheeks at the movement and she looked at his face again. "We have to."

He tilted his head. "Why do we have to?"

"Because I work for you. I can't just sleep with you

and then be forced to be in your employment. That's asking for hurt feelings and issues. Then, of course, you're hurt; and we need to figure out if you can use software for your work or write one-handed or have me help somehow. I don't know. But all of that together means I can't kiss you again. Okay?"

"I'm the one who kissed you," he reminded her, knowing he was pushing.

She shook her head. "I kissed you back."

"We can be adults about this." She moved closer, and he wasn't sure she was even aware of it.

"Adults about what? I'm friends with your family, and I'm in your space more often than not. It won't work, Griffin." She leaned forward and put her hand on the bed next to him. "It won't work."

He raised his free hand and cupped her face. Her eyes widened, and she looked down at her feet before darting a look back at him.

"How...how did I get here?"

He smiled softly. "You walked here on your own. Your mind is saying one thing, your body another. I'm not going to take advantage of you, Autumn, but you have to know you have options."

She swallowed hard, a slight tinge of fear entering her eyes that had him worrying. "I never have options."

"Tell me, Fall. Tell me what worries you."

She pulled away. "I can't." Her voice was cold this time, the emotion she'd had before gone. "Let me put your tray over you so you can eat."

He grunted, unsure of what to do next, what to say. He wanted to know what made her tick, and she kept pulling away. Was she just a novelty to him? A puzzle? He didn't think so, but he didn't want to hurt her if that was all it was. She might be strong as hell, but she also had a fragility about her that not everyone could see.

"Autumn." He reached out and gripped her wrist in a gentle hold.

She flinched, but he didn't let go. Damn it. Something had happened to her, something he couldn't name.

"Autumn," he said again, this time softer. "I'm here if you need me."

"I'm the one who is supposed to be here for you," she said, not looking at him. "You're hurt because of me. You're in pain because of me."

He cursed and pulled her closer to him. She ended up sitting on the edge of the bed, and he sat up so he could rest his forehead on hers.

"Fall."

"I hate that nickname."

"I know. And *never* think this is your fault. It was a

drunk driver who hit us. You could have been *killed* because of him. This was *not* your fault. Understand?"

She leaned into him just a fraction of an inch, and the tension in his shoulders eased ever so slightly. "Your hand, Griffin," she whispered, her voice barely loud enough for him to hear.

"I know. It sucks ass, but we're going to be okay."

She snorted at his words, and he had to smile. "I need to go, Griffin."

He used his left hand to tilt her face toward his, their eyes meeting. "I know. But we're not done here. Far from it." He brushed his lips across hers, once, twice, a bare breath of touch. He kept his eyes open to see her reaction and wasn't disappointed. Her pupils dilated even as worry and heat warred.

He had no idea what he was doing, nor did he know why he was doing it, but he *did* know he couldn't stop. He needed this woman, needed to know more about her—just needed *her*.

And soon he'd figure it all out. Because if he didn't, he had a feeling they'd both be broken in the end. He'd been left broken once before, and he wasn't sure *either* of them would survive if they had to break again.

CHAPTER EIGHT

Why Autumn had said yes, she had no idea. Perhaps she'd gone insane. Or maybe she'd been the one who'd hit her head in the accident and not Griffin. How she'd ended up in the middle of a Montgomery family indoor BBQ in a semi-fancy dress and heels, she'd never know.

It had been three days since the accident, and other than Griffin's hand, the two of them were almost back to normal in terms of their health. Normalcy in terms of anything else had gone so far out the window, she didn't even remember what their version of normal looked like.

He hadn't tried to kiss her again, and she hadn't leaned into him, wanting that kiss. Of course, she *wanted* that kiss, but craving something bad for her was par for the course these days. Griffin was her boss, brother to her friends, nothing more.

And if she kept saying that, maybe she'd actually believe it, rather than doing something like, oh... coming to his family meal. In a dress.

Seriously, what the hell had she been thinking?

"Why are you frowning like that?" Griffin asked as he walked up to her side. He held a drink in his non-casted hand and held it out to her. "I got you a lemonade since you're driving us home." He winked as he said it, and she held back an eye roll.

His home, she reminded herself. Not hers. Contrary to what her hormones wanted, she hadn't slept at his place since that first night. Storm had replaced her battery so she could drive where she wanted to and chauffeur Griffin around when he didn't have one of his countless family members doing it for him.

"Thanks," she said as she took the lemonade from him. "What about your drink?"

He grinned as Storm walked over with a drink for his brother. Storm snorted then did that chin lift thing guys did. "Now I have my drink."

"But...but why didn't you just keep that one and let Storm give me the extra one in his hand?"

Storm snorted again. "Need some allergy meds, bro?" Griffin asked. "And I wanted to get you your drink, and rather than risk my mother's carpets, I asked Storm to help."

She did not understand men. She *really* didn't understand Montgomery men.

"You're weird, but whatever."

"You like me that way."

Storm snorted. Again.

"Seriously, do you need something for your nose?" Griffin asked, and Autumn held back a laugh.

"I'm fine," Storm said casually. "Just enjoying the show."

Autumn narrowed her eyes. "There's no show."

"Sure there isn't, hon." The man winked.

"Don't call her hon," Griffin said. "She prefers Fall."

She closed her eyes and prayed for patience. Most days, Griffin was tolerable, but put him in a room with his brothers when he's in a mood, and suddenly he's a little kid again, bent on torturing all those in his vicinity. If only she could make her drink stronger.

There were so many sides to Griffin. There was the fun one that teased her and his siblings. The overprotective one that had apparently punched Decker for daring to touch Miranda. The dark and broody one, who emptied himself into the pages of his book. Then there was the possessive one, who took her by the hair and plunged into her mouth, making her ache and beg him for more.

It was enough to make her head spin.

"I think you've made her head hurt," Storm said, interrupting her thoughts. He smiled at her, his eyes filled with laughter. "I don't know how you work with him every day. You're a stronger person than I am."

"I'm not that bad," Griffin added in.

She bit her lip and winked at the man who kept invading her thoughts. "Oh? Uh...as my employer is standing right next to me, I should probably only say nice things."

Griffin huffed but leaned closer to her, his breath warm against her neck. "You like coming to my home now, don't you? It's not like it was before."

She couldn't help shivering from his nearness, and she knew Storm hadn't missed the encounter either. One eyebrow rose high, but the other man didn't comment. Thankfully.

"What are we talking about over here?" Wes asked as he came up to them. Storm's twin grinned and ran a hand down his tie. She loved that the twins were so different, though it seemed as if they held a special bond that none of the other Montgomerys had. Or rather, an additional bond since she'd never seen a family as close as them.

"About Autumn's fortitude," Storm said easily.

"For working with Griffin? Yeah, I would say she has nerves of steel, but that would be rude to our dear baby brother."

Griffin flipped them both off, and this time, it was Autumn who snorted.

"Watch your language!" Meghan snapped from her corner with Luc. They weren't making out—yet—but they were leaning on one another like they couldn't wait to get alone.

"I didn't curse!" Griffin called.

"Finger gestures count, man," Luc said, not taking his eyes off Meghan.

Those two needed to get married already.

Meghan's two kids from her previous marriage—Sasha and Cliff—giggled from their spot on the floor as they played a game with Austin's son, Leif. Austin and Sierra's baby, Colin, was sleeping happily in his grandmother's arms near them. Harry sat in his large chair, watching his grandchildren with an odd smile on his face.

Autumn narrowed her eyes at the man. There was something different about him, but she couldn't quite place it. It wasn't as if she truly knew him, but there was something...changed at least. It also wasn't her place to say anything, so she pulled her gaze from him and the children and turned back to Griffin as he spoke to the twins about some Montgomery Inc. project.

"You're not allowed to help," Wes said quickly. "Your hand."

"I still have another hand," Griffin explained.

"It's not about that, bro," Storm said. "Come on. You remember the incident with the saw, don't you?"

Autumn's eyes widened. "Saw? Oh my God. What did you do?"

Griffin winced. "We don't talk about the Incident." He turned to his brothers. "And I'll thank you for not bringing it up every time I want to help."

"You have your own deadline, Griffin, we'll manage ours," Wes said, not unkindly.

She felt Griffin's wince this time, though he didn't actually show it on his face. She knew he'd been working more before the accident, but since, he hadn't written a word. He'd been healing under her care, but tomorrow they would have to find a new routine. There was no way they could put it off any longer.

"Are you annoying Griffin again with the Incident?" Miranda asked as she leaned into Decker. The two looked as if they didn't match—her with her dainty features and school teacher smile, him with his bearded, broody look and tattoos covering his body—

but the way they looked at one another, there was no doubt they were perfect for each other.

"We're not discussing the Incident," Griffin bit out.

Now she really wanted to know, but she wouldn't ask in a group like this. She'd wait until they were alone so she didn't end up embarrassing him. Why would she go and think of them alone? This wasn't good for her brain...or her heart.

"Did someone mention the Incident?" Austin asked as he came over, his hand firmly tangled with Sierra's.

"Really, boys, stop making fun of Griffin," Sierra said with a smile. Her long chestnut hair trailed in waves over her shoulders and looked as if someone with large hands had pulled at the masses ever so slightly. Go, Sierra.

"Yes, stop making fun of me," Griffin said with a smile. "And now that you're all gathered, I'm going to go take Autumn on a tour of the house." He handed his drink off to Storm, who of course snorted, and took Autumn's free hand in his own. "Come on."

"No making out in your old room!" Decker called, and Autumn blushed.

"I can't believe you just did that," she whispered as he pulled her into the hallway where no one could see them. "Now people think we're going to make out or something. I work for you, writer boy."

He smiled at her, and her heart clenched. It wasn't supposed to do that. Her heart was supposed to remain firmly in her chest and get in line with her mind. Only her mind kept giving her images of Griffin over her, under her, and behind her, using his one good hand to show her just how talented he was.

Damn it.

"I like the blush on your cheeks, Fall. You going to tell me what you're thinking about?"

"I'm thinking about the Incident."

He narrowed his eyes. "No, you weren't. And no, I'm not going to tell you about the Incident. You should really tell me what you were thinking." He cupped her cheeks, and she licked her lips.

"What are you doing?" she breathed.

"What do you think I'm doing?" he asked, lowering his head. His breath warmed her lips, and all she had to do was tilt her head up ever so slightly and she'd feel his mouth on hers.

She didn't move.

She couldn't.

"Making a mistake," she whispered. "You're making a mistake."

He frowned at her but didn't pull away.

"We're in your parents' home, Griffin." She swallowed hard. "Let me go, please."

He pulled away then took a step back, clearing his throat. "You're right. This isn't the place, isn't the time."

"There can't be a good place or time, Griffin."

He tilted his head, studying her face. "Are you sure about that?"

No. Not at all. But she couldn't say that, could hardly even think it.

"What are you doing, Uncle Griffin?" Sasha asked, startling Autumn.

She turned toward the little girl and tried to smile. "Hi, Sasha. I thought you were playing with your brother and cousin."

"I need to go potty, and you're standing in the way," she said with a smile. "Were you going to kiss Uncle Griffin?"

Autumn closed her eyes. "No. No, I wasn't."

"Okay." Autumn opened her eyes again as Sasha skipped by them and closed the bathroom door behind her.

"Well, that went easier than it could have," Griffin said dryly. He leaned against the wall opposite her and smiled.

He hadn't shaved since she'd first started working for him, and now his beard was more than scruff and right at the point where he had to comb it every morning. She never knew she had a beard fetish, but damn she wanted to run her hands through that beard and rough it up some so she could feel it against her skin.

He raised his brows at her, and she let out a breath.

"Let's go see your family," she said instead of petting him like she wanted to. She was stronger than that. Maybe. "Though I still don't know why I'm here. This isn't one of your normal BBQs from what I hear. I only see family."

He shrugged. "Maya will be here with Jake. You aren't the only one who isn't family. And I wanted you here. My parents wanted you here."

She didn't know what to think about that. "But aren't Maya and Jake an item or something like that?"

"They keep denying it, and Mom said Jake is bringing his girlfriend." He lowered his brows then, and Autumn blinked.

"Jake has a girlfriend. How do we not know that?"

"I didn't know until Mom mentioned it. It's apparently getting serious or something. That's why she wanted the girl here. Or maybe she wants the girl here so Maya can see what she's missing. I don't know."

Autumn shook her head. "Your family confuses me."

"Welcome to the Montgomerys. Come for the ink and food, stay for the drama."

She smiled as they made their way back into the

living room that had gone quiet. As soon as Autumn's gaze drifted to the foyer she knew why.

Maya and Jake had arrived.

Along with an adorable blonde in a very cute pink and white dress.

The difference between this blonde and the way she looked, and Maya's skinny jeans and black tank top showing off her ink and piercings as much as possible couldn't be more prominent if they'd been standing side by side.

The fact that Jake stood between them, looking oblivious, just made it more awkward.

Maya glared at her family as if willing them not to make a remark that could hurt her. Or knowing Maya, that could hurt Jake.

"You brought Holly, Jake," Marie Montgomery finally said as she handed off her grandbaby to his mother. "I'm so happy you did. It's about time we met the woman stealing our Jake's heart."

Holly blushed right to her pale blonde roots, and Jake wrapped his arm around her shoulders. Maya stared at him as if she'd never seen him before, but she didn't look hurt...didn't look jealous. She just looked... different. As if the other woman didn't know what to do now that her best friend had someone to hold.

Maybe the Montgomerys had been wrong and

Maya and Jake weren't for each other. Maybe they didn't love each other the way they all thought. Maybe this would work out.

Or maybe someone would end up broken in the end.

And that was just another reason Autumn couldn't fall for Griffin or the Montgomery family. When she had to leave—and that was any day now—it had to be quick. Painless. She couldn't leave so many strings, so many connections.

She knew it was too late for some pain, but the agony could be held off.

She prayed, at least.

Marie hugged Jake close, then did the same to Holly. The young woman's eyes widened for a moment, then she hugged Marie back.

"Thank you so much for inviting me," she said softly. "I know this is a family thing, but Jake and Maya said it would be okay since you wanted me here."

"We don't bite. Much." Maya winked at Holly and smiled.

Autumn met Griffin's eyes. He just shrugged, and she let out a breath. Well, at least dinner would be interesting. Of course, she knew it would have been even without the Holly/Jake/Maya drama. The Montgomerys knew how to intrigue her just by breathing.

Hence why she should be ready leave as soon as she found a place to go.

"Well, it's good you're here," Marie said. "I'll introduce you to everyone, and then we can all come and gather around the couches. Harry and I have something we'd like to say." She smiled softly, and Autumn felt Griffin stiffen beside her. "I didn't know we'd be announcing this today, but I'm glad you're here since you're part of Jake's life."

"What's going on?" Maya asked.

"Go sit down, darling. We'll explain in a moment."

Autumn looked over at Harry, who leaned back in his recliner as Marie introduced Holly to the rest of the Montgomerys. They all looked as shell-shocked as Griffin. Between Holly and now this mysterious announcement, it was a lot to take in.

"Tell us now," Austin said as he pulled Sierra onto the couch next to him. Leif sat on the floor, leaning into his dad's legs.

"Yeah, what's wrong, Daddy?" Miranda asked. Decker sat next to Sierra and tucked Miranda on his lap, running his hand over her back.

"Are you having to get more treatments?" Meghan asked. She sat on the other couch next to Luc. Both kids piled onto the couple's laps and held hands. They were old enough to know that something was off...or least that something was coming.

"Just tell us already," Wes said. He leaned against the couch, Storm next to him. The other twin didn't speak, only frowned at his father.

Maya sat next to Luc as Jake and Holly took the empty seats next to her. Her shoulders stiffened for the barest of moments, and Autumn wasn't sure anyone else had caught it but her.

Griffin took Autumn's hand, and she squeezed his. They hadn't moved from the hallway, but with the way the living room was situated, they were still in the center of it all. Autumn couldn't help but think that she, Holly, and perhaps Jake shouldn't be there right then. But even as she thought it, Griffin tugged her close. She shuffled to his side and let him lean on her just a little. If he needed her there, then she'd be there. But she'd have to do her best to stay strong against him.

She looked over the Montgomerys and knew she'd never again see such a close-knit group. They loved each other even through the worries and pain that came with life. The fact that they were missing one of their own wasn't lost on her either. Alex should have been there, and she hoped one day he would be. He needed to heal himself first.

"Dad," Austin growled out the word, and the others quieted down.

"I went to the doctor yesterday for my appointment," his dad said smoothly. "As of that appointment, I'm officially in remission. I can't call myself cancer free until I reach a certain time, but I'm well on my way."

It was so quiet she could have heard a pin drop. Everyone held his or her collective breaths until it was as if someone had punctured the vacuum. People jumped up, hugged, yelled. Others cried, holding on to one another and their father. The kids danced around, giggling for their grandfather.

Yet with all of the chaos, Autumn only had eyes for one man.

Griffin kept his gaze on his father, who gave him a small nod. He shook slightly, and Autumn put both hands on him, making sure he was okay.

"Griffin?"

He fell to his knees, pushing her against the wall as he put his head on her stomach, his arms going around her waist and butt.

"Thank God. Thank God."

Tears soaked her dress, and she lowered herself to the floor as much as he would allow, running her hands down his back and through his hair.

"He's okay," she whispered. "He's okay."

He nodded against her shoulder, placing his face between her neck and chin and held her tight. At that moment, she didn't care what they looked like, what others would think. She only cared that this man held so much inside, so much on his shoulders, that he'd broken just a bit—broken to the point that he needed to let it all out.

She let him cry, let the others celebrate and allow their emotions to come out however they needed to. She'd care about the rest of the world later. Right then, it was all about Griffin. All about the man in her arms.

And soon she'd figure out what all of that meant.

Soon.

MAYA

This wasn't the first time she'd eaten a meal with Jake and a woman he was sleeping with. This *was* the first time Maya didn't know what to do with her hands, didn't know what to do with her words.

She didn't like this feeling. Didn't like the way she couldn't figure out what to say next or do when it came to this sweet girl named Holly.

Maya didn't hate Holly. Not in the slightest. There was nothing to hate about Holly. She was nice, compassionate, and truly cared about Jake. As Jake was Maya's best friend, Maya couldn't ask for anything more in a woman for him.

Sure, Holly didn't have a single tattoo on her, and probably only liked missionary with the lights off, but if that's what Jake wanted, then more power to him. It wasn't Maya's job to worry about Jake's lovers.

Only this time, Maya couldn't help but feel different.

Jake wasn't just sleeping with this woman. He was *falling* for her.

Things were getting serious. He'd introduced Holly to his family, the crazy Gallaghers who rivaled the Montgomerys in drama and ink. And now he'd introduced Holly to the Montgomerys. Maya had a feeling that soon, Jake would get down on one knee and make Holly his in truth and forever.

Maya should be happy for him. Because despite what her family thought, she'd only ever loved Jake as her best friend. She'd never allowed herself to think about him as something more. As soon as she did that, she'd lose him forever. It was what she did. She fucked a man then fucked it up royally. She'd rather have Jake as her best friend, who she never slept with, than have him for a night or two and lose the one man she could tell anything to.

But...but something was wrong.

Her heart hurt.

She rubbed her hand over her chest as Jake and

Holly laughed about something they'd seen at the park. Maya forced a smile, and she knew Jake didn't see it. If he'd been paying attention to her and not the woman she had a feeling he loved, then he'd have seen the strain, seen the lie.

But he didn't see.

He only saw Holly.

And that had to be good enough.

Because this was *not* jealousy she was feeling.

Not at all.

Maya Montgomery did not love Jake Gallagher.

Jake was her best friend. Not the man she'd grow old with.

Jake would be with Holly, and Maya would be...

Maya would be okay.

Because she had to be.

CHAPTER NINE

Writing sucked ass.

Griffin wanted to slam his head against his desk once again but stopped himself. Mostly because Autumn was staring at him and he didn't want to look like an idiot. Since the accident, he'd done everything he could on the other side of writing so he didn't actually have to try and type. Contrary to popular belief, writers didn't normally light a candle and type in one sitting until a polished manuscript appeared. It wasn't like Jim Carrey typing on his computer in that one movie where he played a man with God's powers for the week, manically slamming his hands on the keyboard until words appeared.

Griffin couldn't slam much of anything with his broken hand. He knew the hand he'd held out from his body had been to try and protect Autumn, and it wouldn't have helped in that kind of collision no matter what he'd done, but he probably would have done it again. He didn't want her hurt. Couldn't even think it.

And he'd have to dive deeper into those thoughts and emotions later because there was no way he could do it with her in the room, looking at him with abject pity. The fierce resolve mixing with the pity in her eyes, though, worried him more.

She wanted to fix this, and would have probably written the book herself if she could. No matter how many times he told her the accident wasn't her fault, she didn't listen. She blamed herself, and the longer he sat looking at his keyboard like it was the enemy, the worse she would feel.

Hence why Griffin needed to fix this. Now.

"We will figure this out," Autumn said softly.

He turned to look over his shoulder and lifted one side of his mouth in a semblance of a smile. "Yeah, we will." He stared back at his keyboard that mocked him with all its precious keys. "Somehow."

"You can always type one-handed..."

He snorted then smiled at her again. It must have come out as a grimace because she winced. "I could try, but that's a lot of hunting and pecking on a deadline. It's not off the table, though."

"And you're right handed, so writing by hand is out, too."

He nodded. "Yep." And even if he could write it out, someone would have to type it, and he wasn't sure if he liked the idea of anyone—especially her—seeing his book in its raw form.

"What about dictation software? That would save your hands. And I think you just have to download it."

He blew out a breath. "I actually already have it and have tried it a few times to try and save my wrists." He turned in his chair to fully face her. "It's a mess. I spend more time editing what the thing thought I said rather than what I actually said. It's horrible for fiction, honestly. It censors any cursing or sex I have in the book, and it never gets the names right. Plus the hes and shes are fucked over. But it's better than staring at a blank screen and missing my final deadline."

Autumn pressed her lips together before speaking. "You can try that for a bit...and I can be the software too if you want."

He frowned. "Huh?"

"You can dictate to me. I'll type for you. You just have to say what you want me to write. I know it will be hard, but I understand the names and cursing and everything like that. I promise I won't judge or change anything you want to write. I'll be your hands if you'll let me."

He sat back in his chair and let his gaze fall to his cast. She wanted to type for him? He hadn't even thought of something like that, and on the outside, it sounded like the perfect solution. From the inside, though, it was as if he were baring his soul for her to see every little bit of him. He wasn't sure he could do that, show her who he truly was through his words. But he did that every day with his books anyway, didn't he? Only readers didn't know that. Didn't know that each time he put his characters through the wringer, he was doing it to himself, as well. Each time he kept his characters on the run, he was running right alongside them, out of breath and lost until the next action came along.

Could he let Autumn see that part of him?

Did he have a choice?

"Forget it," Autumn said quickly as she stood, running her hands over her skirt as if straightening the nonexistent creases. "I shouldn't have said something like that since you're so private about your work as it is. The hunting and pecking might be your best bet at this point." She turned to walk out, and Griffin cursed under his breath.

"Wait. Come back. I was just thinking about what you being my hands would mean. I wasn't pushing you away. Sit for a minute. Okay?" He gestured toward his thinking chair, rather than the one she'd sat in before. "You can even sit there, it's more comfortable anyway. And maybe it'll help us figure this out truly."

She narrowed her eyes, studying his face, then slowly made her way to his lush, leather thinking chair and sat down on the edge primly.

He didn't want to think about how hot she looked just then, all prim and proper with a mix of hippy nomad thrown in for good measure. He wanted to bend her over that chair and fuck her hard until they both were a pile of limbs on the leather, sweaty and begging for more.

"It could work..." he said slowly. "But it won't be easy. I've never...I've never put my thoughts out in the air like that. They always go straight to the page, you know?"

She relaxed some, letting her hands fall to her sides and she leaned into the plush chair. "I know. That's why I saved that idea for last."

He snorted. "Well, thanks for trying to spare my feelings at least."

"I try."

He smiled fully then, even though his career was rapidly spiraling away from him and he didn't have the hands to hold on for dear life.

"I don't know how to dictate my book, Autumn. I don't even know how I write. It just...happens." He frowned. "No, that's not right. I outline if I can and plot out story arcs and pray it works. And then I sit at the computer and usually let the words fall from me. It's a job, not a passion. Or not just a passion. This book has just been harder than the others for some reason."

"Maybe because you were so worried about what would happen if you didn't do your job, you ended up not doing it anyway."

"That had something to do with it."

Autumn licked her lips, and he grew hard at the sight of her cute pink tongue darting out over her plump mouth. She swallowed hard, and he met her gaze. She wanted him and was fighting it. Well, damn, he was fighting it, too. And once he opened his world, opened his words to her, it would make wanting her in his bed that much trickier. It might be worth it, though.

"Um...why don't you start talking about what book you're working on and maybe that will help?"

"You don't sound so sure." He leaned forward, the scent of her lotion making him want to taste, to touch.

"It's the first time I've done this, you know."

"How about you tell me about the book you're reading."

She frowned. "What does that have to do with anything? That book has nothing to do with yours."

"Not necessarily true. I want to know how your brain works, how you like your books. And maybe talking about books, in general, will make it easier for me to talk about my own in a capacity behind a shielded interview."

"Fine. I'm reading a romance. I love romances. Love watching two—or sometimes three—people find their way through the world, through pain and sacrifice, through everyday things to a happy ending."

He smiled. "I read romances too, Autumn. They aren't just a woman's game."

Her eyebrows shot up. "Say what? You don't write romances."

"True. I find it harder to get to the happy ending, and like the thriller suspense act a bit more when it comes to what I write. But I read every genre I can. Just because I don't write it, doesn't mean I don't respect it."

"But...but you *killed off* a character's HEA."

"Did I?" he asked, genuinely confused. "She wasn't his happy ending, Autumn. He's not at the ending yet. Neither of my main characters is."

"But what if they want to be?"

"Then I'll know it's time to end the series. I'm not there yet." He didn't know if he'd ever be at this rate. He still had to find the path he needed for his current book, let alone the rest of the books for each of his two main characters in his two series.

She let out a breath. "Can I say something and you not get angry?"

He tilted his head, studying her face. "You can say something, but I can't gauge my reaction until you say it."

She smiled a little and bit her lip. Damn that lip, he wanted a bite for himself. "Your characters are always running. Always going from one thing to the next and never standing still for fear of what is coming after them. Do you do that on purpose?"

He froze before forcing himself to relax. "It's a suspense, they need to run. They aren't safe if they stand still."

"I understand that," she whispered, so low he thought he might have imagined the words themselves.

She intrigued him. She always had, and now her secrets were tugging on his writer's brain. He wanted to unveil what he could, unwrap her until she was his...at least for the moment.

She cleared her throat. "Are you ever planning to give your characters a romance that works?" Clearly she didn't want to talk about what she'd just whispered. He'd let it go. For now.

"Maybe. It depends on how things work out for them."

"But they need something, don't they? A connection to that reason why they find the bad guys, why they fight. They need a purpose to go on those missions rather than just to save the world. Right?"

He smiled softly. "True. But that doesn't necessarily mean the purpose will be a romance. Finding themselves is just as important as finding the culprit." And the basis for his series, even though not all understood that. Though now that he truly thought about it, he knew it was more than that.

Why bother solving the thrills, finding those bad guys as she put it when they came home to nothing.

Why bother writing them when he was alone himself...

Lauren filled his mind once more and he blinked. He hadn't thought about her in years, and yet he'd thought of her twice in as many weeks.

"What put those shadows in your eyes?" she asked, her voice soft, hesitant.

He cleared his throat. She'd be seeing inside him soon enough when he opened his mind for his book. He may as well tell her.

"I was actually thinking of Lauren."

She pulled back, a look of pain on her face for a mere moment before she carefully masked it.

Fuck.

"Lauren was my girlfriend in high school. She died of cancer right after graduation. She wanted to be an editor for a big publisher and live the city life. That wasn't what I wanted, but I figured I could have worked with it. We were young, but hell, my siblings had gotten married and all that at my age." He met her gaze, folding his hands in front of him as he leaned on his thighs. "The fact that both those marriages are done for now hasn't escaped me."

"You loved her."

"I loved her as much as I could have as a teenager. I don't know if it's the same love as an adult. I haven't been in love as an adult. That could be a reason I don't write about my characters being in love since I've never felt it at their ages. But I also don't chase down terrorists and defuse bombs on a daily basis, so it's not the 'write what you know' bullshit. I'm getting sidetracked." He let out a breath. "The cancer came on fast and hard. She was diagnosed before prom and died that summer. I don't know if we would have made it as adults, but I do know we never had a chance. That's what I was thinking about. How I don't have the romance or HEA that you think my characters deserve."

"You miss her," she whispered, her eyes set on his. There weren't tears in them, but he saw the emotion.

"Yeah. She was my friend. Decker was my best friend, still is, even though we've grown up and grow into our lives. But Lauren was my friend. My first for a lot of things. And now she's gone, and it sucks that she didn't get a chance to experience life." He scrunched his face. "It sucks she never got to read a book I got published."

Autumn stood up and walked toward him. He leaned back and stared at her as she stood between his legs, her hands trailing up his arms as it looked as if she were deep in thought.

"I'm sorry for making you remember."

He shook his head. "Don't be. I'd rather remember than forget her. She deserved more than that." He gripped Autumn's wrist with his uninjured hand. "I didn't mention her to tell you she was the one for me and that I haven't been with another since because that would be a lie. It's been over a decade. She may have shaped who I was, but she hasn't shaped who I am now. I honestly don't know why I thought of her then, except we were talking about lost happy endings. She was a lost happy ending, but hopefully, she won't be my only chance at that happily ever after."

Autumn cupped his face and studied him. He let out

a breath, wanting more of her gentle hold. Here he was, talking about Lauren when all he wanted was Autumn. He should have felt ashamed, dirty, but he didn't. He knew Lauren would have wanted him to move on. And he had in a sense. Only he didn't know what he was doing now—in life or with his words. Maybe that was the problem. Maybe that's why he kept thinking of a girl long since gone. Because he'd thought he'd known who he was back then. Perhaps now it was time for him to figure out who he was again.

Who he was with Autumn.

He slid his hand up her hip over her dress and let it settle there. "I want to kiss you again, Autumn. Are you going to be okay with that?"

She nodded. "I think I'm okay for more. It's beyond stupid. I need to help you with work…and I won't be here for long, Griffin." She stared at him intensely. "I never stay anywhere for too long."

His hand tightened on her hip and he forced himself to relax it. "I wish you'd tell me why. I wish you'd tell me the secrets in your eyes."

She shut them, her jaw tightening. "I can't."

"Then can you give me what you have to give? Give me what you need? Because I'll take that, Autumn. I want you, you know that. I've wanted you from the start, and I'll do my best not to hurt you, not to let what happens from here on out interfere with what needs to happen with other things in our lives. But you need to tell me you're okay with that. You need to tell me you want me too, and that you know that once you walk away for good, that you won't hate me for it."

She opened her eyes and lowered her head. "I can't hate you for what is out of your control. I can't hate you for running, because, in the end, it will be me that goes."

He didn't know why that hurt, but he pushed it aside like he had all the other times words had hurt. Words were far more powerful than most believed. That's why he wrote them. He'd be with Autumn in this time, in this place. And when it ended, he'd store the memories where he stored those that were just for him, not for his books, not for his worlds. If only she'd tell him why she ran, why she kept her secrets. But she wasn't in a place to tell him, and for now, that would have to do. He didn't know what would happen after, what would happen once she opened her eyes fully and saw him for what he was, what he had to give, but he'd take everything he could.

"No more talking," Griffin whispered. "Not tonight."

She shook her head. "No strings, Griffin. This isn't

about what you lost, what you think I'm hiding. This is just us."

"That I can do, Autumn. Now lean down a bit. I want to taste your lips."

With that, she did as he asked and leaned forward, pressing her lips to his. He groaned at the contact, the hand on her hip tightening once more. She opened for him, sliding her tongue along his. He pulled her closer so she pressed her legs to the chair and his thighs encased her. His hand slid around her hip to her ass, squeezing and molding.

He pulled away from her touch, taking a deep breath. "Sorry I'm one-handed, Fall," he said on a laugh.

She kissed the side of his mouth, his jaw, then behind his ear. He let out a strangled moan as her hand slid down his chest and she gripped him through his jeans.

"I have two hands, Griffin. More than enough, I hope. And I bet you can use that one hand and that sexy mouth of yours to make me come more than once tonight. What do you say?" She bit her lip then leaned forward again to bite his.

His hips rocked up into her hand, even as his own hand played with her thong through the skirt of her dress.

"I say fuck yeah. I love your mouth, Fall. Love the way it looks when you bite into it, love the way it feels along mine. I love the way it looks when you say those fucking dirty things. I'm especially going to love it when it's wrapped around my cock."

She licked his lips and pulled back. He loosened his hold on her to allow her to straighten. "What about your lips on my cunt? Are you going to help me with that?"

He took his good hand and rubbed it along his jean-clad cock. "I think I can do that. Since I'm one-handed, why don't you strip for me? Slowly."

She cupped her breasts and tilted her head. "I think I can do that," she said, repeating his words. "Are you going to watch?"

He met her gaze. "For however long you let me, Autumn. For however long you let me."

CHAPTER TEN

Autumn slowly pulled up her dress, exposing her panties and bra-covered breasts. She did it slowly, achingly slow, so she could watch the way Griffin's gaze traveled from her stomach, up to her breasts, down again a bit lower, then back to her eyes. From the quick intake of breath, she knew Griffin watched her, wanting, needing. She'd never felt so powerful, so sexual.

She tossed the garment over the edge of his spare chair and bit into her lip again, knowing he liked that. She'd seen the way his eyes had darkened before when she bit. She *knew* he liked it. The fact that he'd told her blatantly that it made him hard just made her want to bite even harder.

She wanted to bite him, wanted to lick him up,

every inch of him. She wanted to feel him deep within her, pounding inside her until they were both overcome and spent. The real thing couldn't be as powerful as her fantasy, as intoxicating, but for some reason, it was perfect—too much and not enough all at once. Just the thought of him, in fact. She was like Goldilocks with her three choices, and yet she wanted them all.

And the man wasn't even touching her.

Yet.

"I love your curves, Fall. Your hips are perfect handholds for me." He grinned a little sheepishly. "Well, one hip will be. If I had two hands, then...well..." He cleared his throat. "Now where was I? Oh, yeah. Your curves. I love your stomach, so soft yet firm at the same time. I'm going to enjoy licking up every inch, finding your taste and lapping up your sweetness."

She tilted her head and put her hands behind her back, her fingers playing with the clasp of her bra. "Just my stomach? That's all you want to taste?"

He stood up, then—tall, strong, and powerful. He towered over her, but she wasn't scared. She should be. She should run and never look back. But she couldn't. Not with this man, not with this moment.

She stayed put and wanted to know what would happen next.

That was perhaps the most dangerous thing of all.

"I want all of you, Autumn." He met her gaze, and her breath caught in her throat. "All of you."

"For now," she corrected.

He paused a moment. "For now," he whispered then crushed his mouth to hers. When had he gotten so close? When had he put his hand on hers and helped her unclasp her bra? She was so lost in him that she scared herself.

But again, she didn't run. She stayed put.

For him.

For herself.

Her bra fell slightly, only staying up because Griffin's chest was pressed to her own. She wrapped one arm around Griffin's back, falling deeper into the kiss as she put the other over her breasts, sliding between them.

"Let me," he growled and tugged on her bra, leaving her bare against him. Her nipples pebbled against his shirt and she shivered. "So pink," he whispered. "So fucking perfect." He lowered his head and took one into his mouth, sucking and biting until she wiggled against him, needing to press her legs together so she wouldn't come right there without even his hand on her.

"Griffin."

"Fall with me, Autumn. Fall." He licked and nibbled on her other breast while using his uninjured hand to roll her nipple between his fingers. She rocked against him so his jean-clad cock pressed firmly against her panties. Griffin bit down. Hard. And she came, her body heating, her knees going weak. She dug her fingernails into his shoulders, needing something firm to latch onto or she'd fall in truth and not just over the crest of pleasure and temptation.

"You're beautiful when you come," he said softly. "All rosy and gasping." He kissed her neck before licking up her jaw to kiss her mouth. "I can't wait to see you come again."

"I'm still in my panties and you're still dressed," she managed. "There's something wrong with this picture."

He smiled then, his eyes sparkling. "Then I guess we'll have to fix that."

She kissed his jaw, licking at the beard there. Damn, she loved his beard. This beard fetish of hers was getting out of control. "I want you inside me."

He kissed her again, this time harder. "One thing first."

Before she could protest, he had her panties off and her butt in his thinking chair. He knelt between her legs and licked his lips.

"Griffin..." She squirmed, her bare ass on the leather a little disconcerting at first. "I thought you were going to fuck me."

"I will." He put her calves on his shoulders and bent lower, his face right above her pussy. "But first I'm going to taste you."

She frowned, even though inside she wanted to do a little dance. She loved, *loved* when a man went down on her and knew what he was doing. Of course, not all men knew what they were doing. From the way he'd kissed and licked her breasts, however, she had a feeling bearded and broody Griffin knew how to eat a woman out in spades.

"At least take your shirt off so I can enjoy what I'm looking at," she teased.

"I plan to have you coming so hard you won't care what I'm wearing, but sure, I can do that for you."

He leaned back and her legs fell from his shoulders. He slid his shirt over his head and she swallowed hard. Ink covered a lot of skin and made her want to explore with her tongue. What wasn't covered in ink was smooth and tanned. Of course, he had chest hair that begged for her fingers. She loved a nice chest with just enough hair and a happy trail that led right to a very large cock. She'd seen him shirtless before, of course, but now it was different. Now he was hers, if only for the moment.

"Now, where was I?" He leaned closer again, putting her legs right where they were before. He kissed her inner thighs and she shivered, leaning back into the thinking chair so she could get even more comfortable. She might as well enjoy a very talented tongue from the best position.

His lips skimmed her thighs again before he licked the place where her hips met her thighs—that crease so unbelievably erotic she almost lifted her ass off the chair. Or she would have if he hadn't placed his arm over her stomach, keeping her in place. She tried to wiggle, but the arm on her waist tightened. Damn man.

He slowly licked up her lower lips before using his free hand to spread her wide. She would have blushed, but his tongue on her clit made her lose her words. He ate her out slowly, nibbling and licking until she knew she was so wet that there was no way he wouldn't be able to taste it, to feel it. His beard scraped her inner thighs, sending shivers along her spine and to her nipples. When he licked again, this time biting down softly on her clit, she fell once more.

Autumn's body shook and she tangled her fingers in his hair, not knowing if she was pushing him closer to her cunt or pulling him away so she could breathe. She just wanted to touch him, *needed* to. He lapped her up, letting her come down from her bliss ever so slightly before he sat up.

He met her gaze, then wiped his face with his forearm, her juices leaving a trail on both. She should have been embarrassed; instead, it only made her wetter.

He quickly stood up and shucked off his pants and boxer shorts. She licked her lips at the sight of his cock—long, just wide enough, and hard as hell. His balls hung low, full and looking very heavy. She wanted them in her mouth, wanted to suck and play with them. Only with the look in Griffin's eyes, she didn't think she had the time yet.

Later.

Later she'd have his cock in her mouth and suck him down.

For now, she watched him slide a condom over his length, his eyes darkening as they met hers.

"I only have the one," he said low, his voice a gruff growl. "It was in my wallet. New and ready for us." He grinned quickly. "I had hopes. The rest of the box is in my room. So for now, I'm going to fuck you on my thinking chair and when it's time for round two, we can head to my bedroom. More angles there."

She licked her lips and nodded before standing. He quirked a brow. "Sit down and let me ride you." She cupped his balls and he sucked in a breath. "This way we don't hurt your hand. Later, you can fuck me on my back, on my knees, or any way we both want. For now, let me be on top. You should be the one sitting in your thinking chair, after all."

He cupped her face with his free hand and kissed her, this time slowly. The aching sweetness of it almost broke her, but she let him kiss her; let herself fall into the moment.

The kiss intensified as he maneuvered them around so he could sit. She broke away only long enough to straddle him. His cock pressed against her opening, but she didn't move down, not yet.

She met his gaze and swallowed. He had his broken hand on the back of her head, keeping his gaze on hers. The other was on her clit, slowly stroking her into near-oblivion. She put one hand on his shoulders to steady her, then the other around his cock to guide him in. Their gazes didn't break as she slowly slid down him.

His mouth parted, his pupils dilated as she took him in. Her body shook, his cock too big, but she keep going, knowing he'd fit, that she'd never forget this sensation of feeling perfectly full.

When she was seated, his cock firmly inside her, she paused, trying to catch her breath. Sweat slicked both of them, and she had to take a shuddering breath.

"Move when you're ready, Fall. *Move.*"

She leaned forward and kissed him, a soft brush of

lips that fractured something deep inside her. She once again ignored it, knowing she had to.

When she was ready, she slowly rocked her hips, moving at a steady pace, never letting their gazes break. His hand moved from her head to her hip, to her breasts, slowly, oh so slowly exploring her as they moved together as one. Her head tilted back as he pressed up, hitting her in that spot that most thought was only a myth. He put his hand back on her head and forced their gazes to collide again.

"Autumn, fall with me. Fall with me."

She rocked once more, breaking over the last peak, coming hard around his cock. He shouted her name even as his name left her lips in a whisper. His cock pulsated deep within her, filling the condom, hot and heady.

They were both out of breath, their bodies sweat-slick and spent, and yet she knew they weren't done for the night. Far from it.

Only after this night, she didn't know what would happen, how far she would have to run to find her safe place. She'd never been truly safe, and with Griffin deep within her body and soul at that moment, at that time, she was afraid she might have found the safest place yet.

With him.

. . .

The next day, Autumn ran her hands through her hair and tried not to look guilty. It wasn't easy when her thighs hurt and bruises and love bites covered her body. Griffin hadn't commented on them, only gave her a too pleased look and brushed his lips over hers softly.

He hadn't touched her again.

Instead, they had worked on his book with him dictating to her. It was a slow-going process, but it was at least working. Somewhat. He hadn't brushed against her the way he had, didn't kiss her, not while they were at work. She understood and was grateful. It might not make sense to outsiders to have them act so differently literally in the same office they'd made love in the night before, but it worked for them.

At least for now.

She would see what happened when they decided they wanted to go for round seven.

Yes, seven. That man had worn her out six times the night before. She was surprised she'd been able to wake up so they could work. Things were getting a hell of a lot trickier, but she couldn't regret it. At least not then.

Of course, now she was sitting in Hailey's café, Taboo, and had a feeling she might start to feel *some* regrets. It was girls' night, after all. Meaning there would be Montgomerys and friends of Montgomerys who saw far more than they should.

They would *know*.

So she would have to find a way to hide it. Somehow.

"You're here!" Miranda threw her arms around Autumn's shoulders and hugged her close. "I was afraid Griffin would have you locked up in his tower while he worked on his book."

Autumn felt her cheeks heat at the memory of Griffin's hand around her wrists, locking her in place as he pumped in and out of her. He'd locked her up all right...

Miranda pulled back and tilted her head. "Interesting."

Autumn raised her chin. "What's interesting?"

"Oh, nothing," the youngest Montgomery said with a grin. "Hailey pulled out all the stops for our girls' night."

Autumn didn't believe for one second that Miranda hadn't seen something on her face, but she let it go. For now. Better to ignore this particular problem for the moment.

"Hey, we can't go out to a bar and drink between the pregnancies and breast feedings, so I thought I'd make lots of baked goods and call it a win." Hailey winked at her, and Autumn smiled back. The other woman's shockingly blonde hair had a purple streak in it today that Autumn figured was hair chalk. She loved the way every woman in the room was unique and held a stamp of their own to mark the world.

Only she wasn't sure who *she* was.

She pushed those thoughts from her mind. It wasn't the time or place.

"I love baked goods as much as they seem to love my hips," Autumn said as she placed her hands on her waist.

"You have great curves, you should own them," Maya said. She sat next to Holly, which still surprised the hell out of Autumn. She not only hadn't expected Holly to be there, but the fact that Maya still seemed okay with the other woman's presence baffled her.

"Oh, I try," Autumn said and waved the other woman off. "They won't stop me from trying that, is that a brownie cheesecake?" Her mouth watered.

Hailey held one out on a small plate. "Come closer, my pretty."

"Temptress," Autumn teased and took the brownie quickly. She bit into the gooey food of the devil and moaned. "Oh my God. I'm dying. I'm actually dying."

"And my plan is complete. Though I wouldn't die yet. I have actual savory food, as well, but I figured we'd go with dessert food first." Hailey paused. "And last. We'll just make a mess of it all."

"I'm fine with that," Callie said with a grin. The younger tattoo artist licked powdered sugar off her lips and closed her eyes. "I swear I'm craving all things sweet *and* savory these days."

"You're pregnant!" Sierra squealed as Callie nodded, and all of the women in the room joined in, clapping and shouting.

Autumn had known there was something different about Callie when she'd last been in the tattoo shop, but she hadn't been able to place it. A new baby. How exciting.

"Morgan must be over the moon," Meghan said as she hugged the other woman. "That man has been waiting an eon for you."

"Did you just call my husband old?" Callie asked with a wink. "He's aged just right, thank you very much." The age difference between the two wasn't *that* bad, but Morgan had to be around forty or so if Autumn remembered. Callie was still in her twenties. It didn't matter in the long run with the way the two cared for each other, though.

Some things were just meant to be.

And Autumn would never have that.

Thoughts of Griffin entered her mind and she

pushed them away. He wasn't for her in the long run. No one was. It was safer if she stayed away. Safer for everyone.

Miranda turned to Hailey and narrowed her eyes. "You totally knew Callie was pregnant before us. You mentioned babies."

Hailey just shrugged. "I see all. I know all."

Autumn snorted. "Sure, honey."

Hailey narrowed her eyes. "I see more than you think."

Autumn quickly sobered. Best not to anger the woman with sweets.

"I'm so happy for you, Callie," Sierra said softly. "Austin is going to get a kick out of this, too. He thinks of you as a sister, you know."

"And he doesn't have enough of those," Maya said dryly before bumping fists with Miranda and Meghan.

"You can never have enough family," Miranda said with a smile. She froze as everyone stared at her. "I'm *not* pregnant. Decker and I are waiting a bit. I'm still new at my job, and we're enjoying being able to have sex on every surface in the house without having to deal with others."

"My baby sister, everyone," Maya mumbled.

"Jealous?" Meghan asked, a wicked gleam in her eye. "It's hard to have sex on the couch when you have kids, but that's what babysitters and school are for."

Maya scoffed. "Hell, no. I'm just fine." Autumn didn't miss how Maya did her best *not* to look at Holly just then.

"Seriously, though," Miranda continued. "I'm enjoying life how it is with work and things. Oh! Did I tell you? I'm not the new one. We just hired a new teacher." She shuddered. "He's not technically replacing...you know...but it's a start."

They all knew what Miranda was talking about, though no one mentioned it. The woman had been through hell because of a teacher with his sights on her. Autumn knew all too well what that felt like.

She swallowed hard. Best not to think of that.

Ever.

Though in all reality, it was always in the back of her mind.

"So any babies in your future, Meghan?" Callie asked as she ate a cake pop.

Meghan smiled. "Perhaps." She held up her hands as the others spoke all at once. "I'm not pregnant now, but we're not going to wait until after the wedding to try. I'm older than I was with Cliff and Sasha, so you never know."

Sierra held out her hand and gripped Meghan's

tightly. "Just be careful." Meghan kissed Sierra's palm before letting go. Autumn felt out of place, if only for a moment, at the sight of so many women with so many stories entwined. But she'd been invited, and was part of the Montgomerys at least right then because of Griffin and her friendship with Meghan.

Holly was the true new one, but she didn't look out of place. In fact, she looked thrilled to be involved. Sweet and innocent. And happy.

The door jingled open and everyone turned to see Tabby walk in, her hair in a tight ponytail at the top of her head.

"So sorry I'm late. Had a last minute thing at work. Oh, are those cake pops?"

"Are my brothers working you too hard?" Maya asked. "Need me to kick their asses?"

"Nope. I just wanted to get ahead of tomorrow." Tabby grinned and bit into a strawberry cheesecake pop. "Oh my God, Hailey. Can we get married? I know I'll be new at the whole lesbian sex thing, but I'll learn for these."

Autumn coughed up her drink of water as everyone broke out into laughter.

Hailey wiped tears from her cheeks and shook her head. "Tabby, darling, you are sexy as hell, but neither one of us likes pussy. We're hard for cock."

That sent everyone into a new round of laughter. The only one that looked a little uncomfortable was Holly, but Autumn didn't think anyone else noticed except for Maya. The group began talking about their days and little stories that made them who they were. Autumn sat back and listened, doing her best not to contribute much. She enjoyed watching, learning what she could about being normal.

Because Autumn Minor had never been normal.

And she knew she never would be.

CHAPTER ELEVEN

"I never thought I'd see you holding a baby like that," Griffin said as Decker rocked Austin's son to sleep.

The women had wanted their girls' night, so the guys were in charge of the kids. Austin had decided to have everyone over to Decker's place and have them *all* watch the kids. Griffin didn't mind, as he loved his nieces and nephews. It was still a kick in the stomach to see his family have families of their own, though. Everyone was growing up, living their own lives, and sometimes, Griffin felt like he was left behind.

It wasn't time for him to worry about that, though. Now he wanted to live in the moment.

Decker just smiled and kept rocking while standing, swaying back and forth as he hummed a little tune.

Colin gurgled once, and Griffin took a step closer. Decker didn't falter; the big, bearded, inked man holding the tiny baby in his arms like he'd always been there.

Austin grinned from the doorway, leaning on the jam and folding his big arms over his bigger chest.

"He asleep yet?" the proud father asked, his voice low.

"Yeah, I think so," Decker whispered. "You got the crib ready?"

Jake came out from the back room, Sasha on his back, and a grin on his face. "It's ready. Sasha helped me put it up."

"He needs *all* the help," Sasha said primly.

Griffin had to put a hand over his mouth to keep from laughing and waking the baby.

Luc plucked his daughter from Jake's back and kissed her cheek soundly. "You're right about that. Now let's get you ready for bed, as well. You're bunking with Leif and Cliff in the guest room. You okay with that?"

She nodded sagely. "I like sleepovers. Even with boys that smell."

"You're going to have problems when she gets older," Wes said as he walked into the living room, Storm on his heels.

"I don't mind," Luc said with a smile and carried

Sasha toward the back, where Leif and Cliff were already playing fort.

"I wonder if I'm going to have a little girl," Morgan said absently, and Griffin grinned.

He slammed his hand on Morgan's massive back and laughed. "I still can't believe you're going to be a dad."

"You work fast," Austin said with a grin.

Morgan raised a brow and looked all the more like the businessman he was. He may have ditched the suit for a casual button up shirt and jeans, but he was still a little cleaner than the rest of them. It didn't matter that he had the largest ink of all of them on his back, the man just oozed class.

And now he was going to be a father.

It was scary how things changed.

"Not fast enough, some would say," Sloane murmured as he carried chips and dip into the living room. The big man didn't pause as the rest of them rolled their eyes at him. Seriously, the man had been courting Hailey without actually courting her for years, and yet he was the one talking about not going fast enough? Crazy man.

Morgan pushed at Sloane's shoulders, and the two of them fell to the couch, sitting down with sodas in their hands and smiles on their faces. Callie might have been the one to do Morgan's ink, but Sloane had also become friends with the man over time.

Griffin loved seeing the way that each set of family and friends seemed to mix and mingle within their own worlds and the large construct of it all. The writer in him wanted to untangle those threads to study them without ever harming them. The Montgomery in him wanted to relish the fact that his family was here, healthy, and getting happy.

His parents were at home in love and safe.

The women in his life were enjoying their night together.

Alex might not be there that night, in that place, but he'd never lose his spot. No matter how far his younger brother had fallen, Griffin would be there to help him stand on his own. He didn't know how much longer Alex had left in rehab, but hopefully, one day soon, he would be able to visit Alex and see for himself how the healing process was going.

"What's wrong?" Decker asked as he walked toward Griffin. He must have handed Colin off to Austin, because Austin was nowhere to be seen, and the rest of the crew had taken their seats in the living room, shooting the shit and eating way too much junk food for men of their age.

Griffin turned to his best friend and sighed. "Thinking of Alex."

Decker nodded and turned to lean against the wall next to him. "I hate that he's not here. I hate more that he hasn't let anyone in to see him. At least he's talking to Marie and Harry, I guess. That has to count for something."

"Are you going to forgive him for ruining your wedding?" Griffin asked, not knowing where the question had come from.

Decker frowned. "There's nothing to forgive."

"What do you mean? He fucked up the reception and scared the kids. Ended up bloody like Luc."

Luc turned to them at the sound of his name and frowned. Decker waved him off, and Luc nodded after studying them for a moment. He turned back to the conversation at hand, but Griffin hadn't missed the curiosity on the man's face.

Decker sighed. "Alex was hurting. It was only a matter of time before he hit bottom." He paused. "I think that was his bottom anyway. We won't know until he tells us. Miranda and I don't think our wedding was ruined. We got married surrounded by friends and family at the Montgomery place. There was nothing more we wanted. Do we wish Alex hadn't fallen? Yes. Do we wish that nothing was wrong with him? Hell, yes. Do we also wish there was a way we could fix it? Fuck, yeah. But we can't. So we're moving on. I love your sister with every ounce of my being. We didn't need the trappings and the perfection of a sunny day with nothing ever wrong to make it perfect for us. It was our moment. That's all it needed to be."

Griffin met his best friend's eyes, floored at the man's words. He knew Decker loved Miranda, of course. Had seen it with his own eyes in all that Decker did. He'd known that once the two fell in love, Decker had taken a step away from their friendship because that was what happened when there had to be a place made for one's soul mate. He hadn't lost Decker in the slightest, but their relationship had changed. And as it had altered, so had the man before him. He'd been hurt, beaten, and had secrets of his own that no other should hold, but he'd found the one person who could not only heal him but also grow with him until the end of days.

Miranda was that person for Decker, and it killed Griffin that it had taken so long for him to realize it. Oh, he'd known for a while now, had known far longer than the marriage actually, but at first, Griffin had fucked up and punched his best friend. He hadn't trusted the man with his little sister and had almost lost everything because of it.

Griffin didn't have the same temper most of the

Montgomerys did. He was a slow burn that turned into a raging inferno. He'd acted without thinking, and had regretted it ever since.

"I'm sorry for hitting you over Miranda," he blurted. "So fucking sorry I didn't trust you with her. I should have. You're the greatest man I know, Decker. And I'm so fucking happy you guys have a future together."

Decker's cheeks pinked a moment, and the living room grew quiet. Griffin knew all eyes were on them, but he didn't care. Not then.

"I understood why you did it. And you've apologized before. It's over, man. You apologize again, and I might have to hit you just because."

Griffin grinned then, his shoulders relaxing. He hadn't even realized they'd tightened.

"His hard head could probably use it," Austin said with a laugh. "Come in and sit down. We have wings, dip, and soda. I know we usually have beer, but with the kids around and all of us having to drive home soon, it didn't seem like the thing."

Decker rolled his eyes. "Thank you for playing host in my house," he said dryly. "I still don't know why we aren't at your place. You're the one with the crib for the baby."

"We did my place last time. We're going to alternate

from now on. Thank God Autumn is cleaning Griffin's place, or we'd all probably catch something."

Griffin sat down on the floor—the only place left for him—and flipped off his brother with his good hand. "Fuck you."

"No, thanks. I'm taken." Austin bit into a chicken wing and moaned. "I've missed these. Sierra has us on a diet of no fried food. I miss grease."

"You do realize the girls are eating chocolate, cakes, and all that shit right now, right?" Sloane asked. He shrugged as everyone stared at him. "I saw Hailey cooking for tonight. She wanted to fatten everyone up since she knows that no one eats like this usually."

"You sure do like knowing what Hailey is up to," Griffin said casually.

Sloane stared at him. "How's Autumn these days? Finally take the step and get her in bed like you've been wanting to do since day one?"

He lifted a lip in a snarl.

"I'll shut up when you do," Sloane said. "I like Autumn. Don't hurt her."

Griffin clenched his jaw, and thankfully, nobody else chimed in. He didn't want to hurt Autumn—didn't plan to—but he had a feeling they would both be left in pieces once they were through. He didn't know what he wanted, and she wasn't planning on staying.

Fuck. He pushed those thoughts from his brain and listened as the others talked of Morgan's impending fatherhood and the fact that Luc and Meghan were trying for a baby. Things moved quickly, too quickly it seemed sometimes, but he did his best to go with the flow. The Montgomerys and friends were being plucked off one by one.

"I have a question, actually," Morgan said as he leaned back into the couch next to Sloane.

"Huh?" Griffin asked.

"Not for you, but for Wes and Storm. I've been watching the way everyone interacts for a while now, and I think I have the dynamics down. Sometimes people surprise me, but usually I can figure out the ties. What I can't figure out is Tabby."

"What do you mean?" Wes asked.

Storm frowned. "What's wrong with Tabby? She works for us."

"Yeah, and yet I thought she was more to either one of you or both. I can't figure it out."

Griffin choked. "Both? Well, that's something I hadn't thought of." The twins glared at him. "What? I figured one of you were with her, or had been, or were thinking about it."

They shook their heads simultaneously. "Hell, no," they said at the same time then glowered at each other.

"I'm not interested in Tabby like that. She's my friend and coworker. Nothing more." Wes stared at his twin. "Something you want to tell me?"

Storm held up his hands. "I've never even kissed her. I don't see her like that. I love how she keeps us in line at work so I can focus on other shit, but she's not the one for me. Seriously." He turned to the others and glared. "And I'll ask you to stop making it sound like we're in some type of twin ménage. We don't share women. Ever."

Wes shuddered. "Fuck, no. I know Austin's friend Sassy has two husbands, but they aren't related, and... just fuck no. I like one woman at a time. And I'm not sharing with Storm. Ever."

Griffin raised his brows. "I think we got it. Tabby's not for either of you."

"You're sniffing around Autumn, so don't think about going near Tabby," Storm said, pointing his soda at him.

Griffin narrowed his eyes. "I'm not doing anything of the kind. Don't say things like that so it makes it sound like Autumn is nothing but something to prowl around."

The others stared at him and he cursed. "Shut up," he mumbled.

"Anyway..." Jake interrupted. "I don't know what

your problem is with threesomes. They can be nice. Well, I never had a threesome while sharing a woman with one of my brothers, but... sharing a woman, in general, can be hot as hell. Plus, fucking another dude while doing it makes it hotter."

Griffin blinked. He knew Jake was bi since he'd never hid it, but the ménage thing was new.

"What the fuck?" Austin said. "Threesomes? Really?"

Decker snorted. "Not much of one to talk, bro," he said to Austin, and Griffin held his head in his hands.

"This is way too much information," he whined. "Let's talk sports and do nothing. Okay?"

Jake smiled unrepentantly. "Just saying. If you're single, and they're willing..."

"You better not be talking about Maya right now," Wes mumbled. "I don't want to know."

Jake sobered. "I've never slept with Maya."

"So you're talking about Holly?" Griffin asked despite himself.

Jake looked a bit pale and as if he hadn't meant to say all he had. "It was a long time ago. Holly and I are good just by ourselves."

There was an awkward silence, and Griffin wasn't sure what he was going to say to try and make it better. Instead, Sloane kicked the chips slightly toward Jake.

"If we're all done talking about our dicks, I want to talk about this client of mine. Could use the help."

Jake relaxed as the others started to talk about ink and not about kink. Griffin kept his eye on the other man, though. It seemed they all had secrets. Ones that once opened to the world might hurt more than just themselves.

He stayed silent as the others spoke, unsure of what he wanted to say. He didn't know where he was in life, who he was, not anymore. He was just now figuring it out after all these years. Things changed, people changed, and Griffin was learning to change with it.

Instead of his book filling his thoughts like it should have, though, it was Autumn.

The woman would hurt him. He knew it. Hurt him and scar him like no other.

Yet it was all he could do not to go see her, to feel her under him.

Things had changed all right, and he wasn't sure if he was ready to see the result.

JAKE

Jake sipped at his beer and wondered how the fuck he'd ended up here. By here, he meant sitting at his brother Graham's house while his other brothers Owen and Murphy played air hockey in the other room, cursing at each other while keeping the score tied as usual. Neither one of them could get a leg up on the other.

He hadn't planned to come over for a family meal since he'd just had one with the Montgomerys, but as much as the latter wanted to adopt him, he still had a family of his own.

Of course, the reason they wanted him over wasn't just Jake's sparkling personality.

The real reason currently sat snuggly next to him on the couch, laughing at something Graham had said.

The Gallagher brothers laughed when they felt like it, brooded more often than not, and didn't care much about what people thought. They were big, bearded, and tattooed much like the Montgomerys, but sure as hell not as large. Plus, there weren't any sisters to add estrogen to the pool, so they were a bit gruffer.

At least that's what Jake thought.

Maya usually brought in the estrogen when she visited, but she hadn't come with him that day.

Instead, he'd brought Holly.

His girlfriend. The one he actually truly liked and who liked him back. He had a feeling she was well on her way to loving him, and if he gave in to what *wouldn't* happen with…well with… He stopped. No, he wouldn't think about either one of them. He could see himself falling in love with Holly if he gave in. He just had to give.

"I'm going to go use the ladies' room," Holly whispered before kissing his cheek softly. "I'll be right back." She smiled at him before heading to the hallway.

"She's nice," Graham said smoothly as he leaned back in his leather chair.

"Sweet even," Owen said as he walked in, Murphy on his tail.

"Too good for you," Murphy said with a grin.

"I can't argue with any of that," Jake said and tipped back his beer.

"Why didn't you bring Maya, though?" Graham asked. "I thought you two..."

Jake shook his head then drained the rest of his drink, already needing a second. He wouldn't indulge though since he had to drive. And after seeing Alex Montgomery fall...well...it was just better not to.

"Maya and I are friends. And I figured we'd still be friends as I date Holly. She's not here because you said you wanted to meet the woman I'm dating and that's Holly...so, well, you get the idea."

His brothers studied him and he did his best not to think about why he felt on edge, why he felt like he was losing something he'd never had.

Holly was perfectly nice.

Nice.

Perfect for him.

Because, really, he'd done the tortured and chaotic shit before and it didn't work. He needed something smooth and easy. Holly would work for the life he wanted.

While *she* wouldn't.

And *he* didn't want Jake.

So that was that.

His phone buzzed, and he pulled it out of his pocket, the name sending a sharp spike down his spine.

"I need to answer this," he said as he stood up, setting the empty bottle down on the coffee table. His brothers stared at him, but he didn't care. They were always trying to figure him out, and once Jake figured himself out, then maybe the other three could, as well.

He closed the back door behind him and blew into his hands, the cold leeching the warmth from him quickly.

"Hey," he said when he answered. He didn't know what else to say, after all.

"Hey." The deep voice on the other end made Jake's mouth go dry, but then again, it always did. It wasn't the first time Border had called. No, the man called every other week or so. Jake would have thought after all this time he'd get over...this.

But he wouldn't.

And the sweet girl in the room behind him would have to help Jake get over the shit that wouldn't just bury itself.

Because Jake Gallagher wasn't going to keep making the same mistakes he always did. He wouldn't let his wants take over the needs he felt he should have.

So, he'd finish this phone call and put it behind him

before going back in to Holly and seeing the future he knew would be okay for him.

Nobody ever got exactly what they wanted in life, so maybe Jake would find a way to make do. Because Holly would be good for him, and he'd be damned sure to be perfect for her.

She deserved that and more.

And Jake, well, Jake didn't deserve anything.

Not anymore.

BORDER

Border hung up the phone and frowned. There had been something different about that call, but then again, he didn't know why he kept calling anyway. Jake didn't seem to want to talk to him like he used to. In fact, with each call, the other man kept pulling away.

Border didn't blame him, as he'd been the one to pull away first.

He let out a breath and ran a hand over his newly buzzed hair. He leaned back, planting his feet firmly on either side of his bike. It was too damn cold for him to be riding, and soon the ice would make it fucking dangerous, but he had to make it a little bit farther. Once he did, he'd get his truck, hook his bike up to the back, and head home.

Home.

To Denver.

Because he'd been a fucking nomad for way too long, and he hadn't found what he was looking for. Of course, he hadn't known what he was looking for to begin with.

He was ready to go home, though.

Ready to go back to Jake.

Ready to figure out what the fuck he'd messed up all those years ago.

Ready to figure out who the hell Maya was…and why Jake was so damn cagey about her.

It seemed he was ready for a lot of things.

He just hoped he wasn't fooling himself. Because if he were wrong, he'd fuck up everything he had. Or maybe he didn't have anything at all to begin with.

Only one way to know for sure.

He started his bike, made sure his helmet and facemask were secure, and headed out onto the open road.

Unlike the last time he'd done this, though, he wasn't trying to find an absolution that would never come.

Instead, he had a purpose.

A plan.

Or at least a future he prayed he'd figure the fuck out before it was too late.

CHAPTER TWELVE

"That's it. Take it. Take my cock."

Autumn arched her back, taking Griffin deeper. Her hands fisted in the sheets and she moaned when his fingers dug into her hips. He pumped in and out of her, his cock slick with her arousal, filling her up and stretching her more than ever before.

He slid his hand up her spine and took her hair in his fist, forcing her back up to his front. "You like that, Fall? You like it when I fuck you hard? You like when you can barely breathe because you're so fucking full you're about to come on my cock again?"

She wanted to say yes, wanted to say fuck yes, but she couldn't speak. Instead, she reached around and grabbed his ass, her shoulder straining at the movement. He growled, the vibrations going straight to her cunt. Her body shook, so close to orgasm she couldn't see, couldn't breathe.

So. Close.

And then the alarm woke her up.

One eye cracked open while the other refused. Her chest heaved and her body was primed.

Of course, it was a dream. Why wouldn't it be? She'd only slept with the man that one night, and now she found herself dreaming about doing dirty, dirty things with him. All the damn time.

Was it wrong she thought real-life Griffin was even bigger and filthier than dream Griffin?

It was official. Autumn was going crazy. Or perhaps she'd already boarded the crazy train and was well on her way to the asylum where she would keep dreaming of fucking a truly gorgeous man and end up all alone in bed with her panties around her ankles and her hand between her legs.

She absently ran her fingers over her clit and shivered, but she wasn't close anymore.

Damn it.

She slid her hand back up and wiped it on the sheets before kicking her panties away. She needed to shower and get ready to head to Maya's. She'd work at Griffin's in a couple of days since he had her on a schedule where she didn't come over every day. He was in the revising stages of his partial book to make sure he was ready for the next part, meaning he could hunt and peck over the keyboard and she could go about helping the other Montgomerys at her fifteen various jobs around town.

Simple.

And yet all she wanted to do was bend over his lap and beg him to finger her until she came.

Bad Autumn.

Bad.

She let out a sigh and rolled to the edge of the bed, groaning as she put herself on her feet. Her hair stood on end, and sweat slicked her body. When she got nice and sweaty with Griffin it was one thing, alone was another matter. She needed a shower and all the coffee in the world.

Unfortunately, she didn't think she had any.

Griffin's fridge may be stocked and filled to the brim, but she'd forgotten to actually shop for herself. Less than a month with the man and he was rubbing off on her.

She wished he'd rub one off with her...

And that was that.

Time to shower and clean Griffin from her mind. Or at least try to.

With another sigh, she quickly stripped off her shirt since she'd already taken the panties off, and turned on her water to hot. Or at least what passed for hot in this place. It wasn't the best neighborhood, but it had walls and a roof and kept her mildly warm in the winter. Plus the landlord hadn't paid too much attention to her paperwork. Sure her name had been changed by non-legal means, but it could at least pass some muster.

Not with cops, though.

Hell.

She closed her eyes and stood under the spray, willing memories and past misdeeds away. She'd rather think of Griffin and those very talented fingers of his. He might only be able to work one hand at the moment, but that hand was pure magic. She could imagine him behind her in the shower, holding her close to his front, his cock pressed firmly between her ass cheeks. He would have one hand in front of them, keeping himself standing by leaning on the wall. He'd run his hand up to her breasts, cupping them one at a time, pinching her nipples until she screamed for him to do something more.

She mirrored the movement, cupping one breast and imagining it was his hand. He would then slide his hand back down and play with her clit, rolling over it slowly before pinching and rubbing. He'd pump two fingers inside her fast and hard until they were both panting and the wet sounds of the shower and her cunt would fill the air. She fingered herself, thinking only of Griffin and his hands. The warm water slid over her clit and she gulped in air, trying to breathe.

Griffin would lean down and bite her neck before whispering one word. "Fall."

And she fell.

Not literally, thank God, but she came. Hard.

Her knees shook and she had to slowly lower herself to the shower floor so she could catch her breath. Getting herself off in the shower was dangerous business, and it would have been better with Griffin, but with his cast...well...that wasn't the only reason he wasn't in the shower with her.

Distance would do both of them good. She couldn't fall for her boss, the brother of her friends. She couldn't fall for a man she would be forced to leave when she had to.

With that pleasant thought, she stood up again and cleaned herself off, the water long since gone cold. She shivered again, this time not in the good way, toweled herself off once she finished, and dressed quickly. She put her hair in a braid and called it a day. It was too cold out for her to go outside with a wet head, so she put on a knit cap. She didn't have the money to pay for that much electricity when it came to a blow dryer. Thankfully, water came with the rent, or that little escapade with dream Griffin would have been costly.

She quickly piled on the layers, slid her bag over her shoulders and opened the front door only to come to a stop.

Her hands shook, but she did her best not to scream.

A dead bird, a crow or raven from the looks of it, lay on her front porch. There wasn't any blood, but it looked as if it had broken its neck...or had its neck broken. There were many reasonable explanations for this. The bird could have flown into her door and died. Another animal could have killed it elsewhere and dropped it on her porch, leaving no blood.

Or *he* could have found her.

She gripped her bag tighter and moved to the porch, her gaze on her surroundings. She didn't feel him out there, didn't see him, but that didn't mean anything. She hadn't felt him all the other times either...not until it was too late.

Chills spread down her arms and she locked the door behind her before walking quickly to her car. She would not run. He liked it when she ran.

She would go back and bury the bird when she had time. The poor thing deserved at least that much. But she couldn't do it now, not when *he* could still be there. Not when she couldn't breathe right.

Autumn started the car and headed toward Maya's place. Her hands tightened on the steering wheel as she thought of everything in her bag. She had everything she needed in her trunk and her bag. She didn't have to go to Maya's. She could just keep driving until she needed to stop for gas. She could leave Denver and never see the Montgomerys again.

Never see Griffin again.

It would be the smart thing to do.

The safe thing.

But once again, Autumn didn't do the smart thing. She didn't want to leave. And because of that, she just prayed she hadn't signed a death warrant for her friends.

For Griffin.

Griffin tilted his head as he watched the twins talk to another contractor about some piece of wood or something. Honestly, Griffin didn't know as much as he should when it came to Montgomery Inc., but he at least tried to be a good brother and help out once in a while. And when his writing was going well and he needed a morning off to breathe, being here helped him, too.

Of course, no one would let him near a saw, so he usually had to paint things. Or glue things. Or nod as others spoke their thoughts aloud. He didn't mind, really, but at some point, people had to let the whole saw thing go. It had been one time.

"You're thinking about the Incident, aren't you?" Storm asked, a grin on his face. "We're not letting you near one."

"Fuck, no," Decker said as he saddled up to them. He put his hammer in his toolbelt and snorted. "No way he's allowed to go near sharp and pointy things. Miranda will kick my ass."

"She's like half your size," Griffin said dryly.

"And she is mighty." Decker nodded sagely, and the brothers laughed. Miranda was mighty for sure.

"Seriously, though, it's been years," Griffin pleaded. "I won't cut an arm off."

Decker glanced pointedly at Griffin's cast. "You're already one arm down, best not to risk it. I have a nice paintbrush and bucket of paint if you'd like to do the trim in this one room. Or you can take notes for me." He winced. "If you can do that one-handed."

Luc wandered over, holding back a grin. "I'm not allowed to help that much either, and this *is* my job."

"You were shot, Luc," Griffin said. "You're not allowed to lift too many things yet."

Wes ran a hand over his face. "Fuck, we're a regular soap opera here. We have shootings, secret babies, car accidents..." He met Griffin's eyes. "Most of that happened when the others found their wives. So, bro, you have something to tell us about Autumn?"

Griffin raised his chin. "I don't know what you mean?"

"For a man who uses words for a living, you never have much to say about Autumn," Decker remarked.

Griffin shrugged; trying to be casual and knowing he was failing miserably. "She's helped me. A lot. I'm actually getting through my book." In fact, he was getting close to the end. Seriously, he had no idea how she did it. All Autumn had to do was be near him, and suddenly, he could write. He could imagine what his characters needed to do, imagine what path needed to be made.

He didn't know if was her or the fact that she'd cleaned for him, all he knew was that he was starting to *want* her there more than he should. And that was scary as hell. What if when she left—and she would leave—he lost everything? What if he couldn't write anymore once she wasn't in his life?

What if he wanted her for more than a muse, a book lover?

What if he just wanted *her*?

"That's good, right?" Decker asked as he slammed his hand down on Griffin's back. "You needed to get to your deadline, or whatever you were working toward. You weren't telling us, so I'm glad Autumn is helping." His best friend narrowed his eyes. "And don't tell me it's just work with her. I've seen the way you look at her, the way she looks at you. You've slept with her."

The others stared at him, and Griffin lowered his head. He didn't want to talk about Autumn. For some reason, he wanted it to be private. Even in as big of a family as the Montgomerys, he wanted something that was just his, just hers—*theirs*. He didn't know if it would stay private, and fuck, it wasn't really that private now, but if he kept it to himself, maybe they'd get off his back.

"Not any of your business, bro," Griffin finally said.

Decker raised a brow. "Odd thing to say coming from you."

Griffin flipped him off. "I thought you said you were over that."

"Oh, I am, totally. But it's still fun to needle you." Decker frowned. "Don't fuck her over, okay?"

"What do you mean by that?" He and Autumn were

just casual. No strings. He didn't want strings, and she sure as hell didn't. They were just doing what their bodies wanted, and when the time came, she'd leave and he'd keep doing what he always did. He didn't need her, and she didn't need him. That's all there was to it.

"I mean, she doesn't have family from what I can tell, so she doesn't have the big brother to tell the dude she's dating all the things he needs to know."

Griffin opened his mouth to shoot that down, but froze. He didn't know if she had a brother, didn't know anything about where she'd been before she'd seemingly dropped from the sky and into the Montgomerys' lives. He had no clue who she was, and yet no matter how hard he tried to ignore that, he wasn't sure he could. She knew more about him than he'd let others know. He'd even talked about Lauren with her. And yet he didn't know anything about her other than the look on her face when she came.

And if they were keeping it to no strings, that should be enough.

It had to be enough.

Fuck.

He hated being kept in the dark. It wasn't just the writer in him, but the Montgomery, too.

"Thanks for looking out for her, Deck, but we're not anything serious so you don't have to worry."

"Sure I don't," Decker said smoothly. The others had been oddly silent during this exchange, and Griffin didn't know what to think about that. "I care about you, too. So just be careful."

Griffin didn't need to hear this. He needed to let his mind go blank before he went back to work. Maybe he'd make out with Autumn when she came by, but it wouldn't be serious, and he wouldn't have feelings.

"If you're done having a heart to heart, I think I'll head over to Montgomery Ink since you guys seem to be good without me here."

Luc shook his head. "Keep running, Griffin. It'll catch up to you eventually."

He didn't want to know what "it" was, so he tilted his chin at the guys then headed back to his rental car. His insurance company had given him the car until they figured out how much Griffin would get for his totaled one. He probably could have bought another one at this point since he had the money, but he'd had other things on his mind.

Namely his book and Autumn.

And his family, his father...Alex.

It was all too much sometimes.

With a sigh, he headed back downtown and struggled through mid-day traffic and pedestrians who didn't understand that jaywalking was actually a crime.

Between the businessmen with too much self-importance, the college kids who forgot to look up from their phones to pay attention, and the random hipsters who didn't care about crosswalks, Griffin was ready for a cup of coffee or something stronger by the time he pulled into the back parking lot for the employees of Montgomery Ink.

He was cranky, tired, and missed Autumn.

And that pissed him off.

He slammed the car door shut then made his way into Taboo for a cup of coffee first. Hailey stood behind the counter and raised her brow at him before sliding over his favorite hazelnut coffee with chocolate shavings on top.

"How the hell did you know I was coming in here?"

She smiled. "I saw you pull in, glower a bit, and figured you could use your favorite. Was I wrong?" She tilted her head, her expressive eyes seeing far too much.

"Thank you," he said in lieu of answering. He leaned over the counter and kissed her cheek before leaving a twenty on the marble. "Keep it, Hailey. You need to pay your bills."

She rolled her eyes then froze. Griffin frowned and turned to the door that connected Taboo to Montgomery Ink. Sloane stood in the doorway, his massive arms crossed over his chest. His jaw was so damn tight, Griffin was afraid the man might lose a filling.

"Sloane." He tilted his head at the other man and did his best to convey that he wasn't poaching on Sloane's territory. Hard to do, when Hailey was right there, staring at the both of them and technically not *with* the other man. Plus, she was her own woman, and calling dibs on women tended to lead to black eyes for the dude involved.

"Montgomery," the other man growled. Damn. Griffin wasn't a small guy—none of the Montgomerys were—but Sloane was *big*.

Griffin didn't look at Hailey again. He'd already said his thanks, and he honestly didn't want to risk another broken bone. His hand ached like a bitch as it healed, and he figured Sloane could do more damage than a car.

Sloane studied him another moment then turned to the side, letting Griffin pass silently. Griffin let out a breath as he made his way into the tattoo shop and met Austin's eyes. His big brother snorted and shook his head.

"You mess with Hailey again?" Austin asked.

He had one hand on his sketchbook, the other twirling his pencil. The shop wasn't that busy, and Griffin figured it had to be the lull before the storm. The shop's artists—Austin and Maya in particular—were booked for the next couple of years with big projects, and usually had people in and out for the little ones besides. Callie bounced from foot to foot as she worked at the computer, and Maya had her head down, her focus on her sketchbook, as well. Just because they weren't laying ink, didn't mean they weren't working. A lot of prep went into a tattoo when it was larger than a postage stamp, and his siblings—as well as those they hired—were the fucking best at what they did. Hence why Griffin's body had so many tattoos to begin with.

"I said thanks for the coffee." He took a sip and moaned. "Dear God, she's a goddess."

Sloane pushed past him and almost knocked the cup from his hand.

Austin gave Griffin a look that said, "You're a fucking dumbass," but had the grace not to say it.

Sloane closed the office door and Austin snorted. "You're a fucking dumbass, Griffin."

So Austin *didn't* have said grace. Whatever.

"You here for a reason, or are you hiding from Autumn?" Maya asked, her attention on her book rather than him.

"I don't hide from anyone," he said through clenched teeth.

"Sure, honey," Maya said with a smile. "I'm working on a sketch for Autumn right now, actually. You want to see it? I'm sure you could imagine the exact place on her body we're going to put it."

He closed his eyes and refused to look at the drawing. His cock ached, and he knew he had a hard-on in the middle of a fucking tattoo shop because he couldn't stop thinking about Autumn. His sister loved teasing him, but damn it, he didn't want to deal with this.

Instead, he turned on his heel, headed back into Taboo with the laughter rolling behind him, set his cup on the counter, and left the building. He'd go home and write. Or maybe jerk off. He didn't know.

But he couldn't deal with whatever the fuck was going on with him right then. Not when he had no idea what it was, and his siblings were having way too much fun razzing him for being with Autumn. He may not have mentioned he was with her, might not have truly been with her in public other than holding each other at his parents' home after his father had given them all the good news, but everyone knew there was *something* going on between them.

Griffin didn't know what that was, however.

And he was going to have to do his damndest to keep that *something* casual.

No strings, she'd said.

He could do no strings.

Even if it killed him.

CHAPTER THIRTEEN

Autumn adjusted her non-prescription glasses with the clear lenses on the bridge of her nose and held back a grin. Griffin had been in a mood all day, and she was tired of it. She'd shown up that morning and had gotten right to work. He'd spoken of car chases and explosions, all the while staying true to the characters and the emotions deep within. He would lie on his thinking chair or pace around the room, trying to voice the thoughts in his head, and she would type them as fast as he spoke. They'd gotten their word count in, and now she was going to have a bit of fun. He needed fun. Even if he hadn't been writing as much as he should have been before she'd shown up, it hadn't been fun for him. She could see the strain in his eyes when he looked at the date, but knew there was hope mixing in, as well. They were getting closer and closer to the end, and she couldn't wait to see what happened next.

She paused.

The end of the book.

Not the end of it all.

The end of them...whatever *they* were.

Of course, that was true wasn't it?

She pushed those thoughts from her brain and adjusted her glasses one more time. It could be a tremendous mistake to do what she was about to do, but she wanted to try it.

Wanted to try a lot of things with him. She quickly ran her hands down her very tight pencil skirt with the slit in the back. Without that slit, it would be hard to pull the garment over her hips later.

Yes, she'd thought about positions where she'd be on top of him or bent over in front of him while picking out the skirt to pack for that afternoon. Priorities and all.

Her shirt was buttoned up to the neck and covered her all the way to her wrists. She'd have fun slowly undoing the buttons when the time came. Or maybe he'd undo the buttons for her. Her heels weren't the prettiest, but they were tall, black, and screamed Fuck

Me. Not that bad of an outfit when she didn't own much to begin with.

She twisted her hair up into a bun of sorts and stuck two pens inside, praying her hair would let her have this moment. A few tendrils curled down the back of her neck, and a strand or four fell to the sides of her face. It worked with the look she wanted, so she didn't try to put them back in the bun. If she did, her hair would probably fall down and laugh at her.

Griffin was in his office, waiting for her to come back so they could work some more. Oh, they'd work a bit longer, then hopefully they'd have some fun. Because no matter how much work Griffin had left to do, he needed fun, as well.

And damn it, so did she.

If recreating some truly horrible porn with some very hot sex made them have fun, then so be it, she'd bend over and take what he gave her.

She held back a snort. Okay, so maybe she shouldn't have watched *so* much terrible porn to make sure she had the outfit and lines down. It sadly hadn't made her hot until she thought of her and Griffin in those positions. And, well...let's just say she'd had to get herself off in the shower the night before.

Again.

It was going to hurt once she left.

Damn it. Not now.

She raised her chin and strutted back into the office. In her heels, she could only strut.

"Good. You're back." Griffin had his attention on his notes, his uninjured hand in his hair as he tugged on it. He looked so damn sexy with that longer on top, short on the sides look. She couldn't wait to have her hands in his hair.

She stood in front of the desk and bent over a bit, playing with a pen. "I'm here," she said, her voice purposely breathy.

Autumn could tell the moment he looked up. His breath caught in his throat and he did that little growl thing, that, when done between her legs, made her come practically on command. As it was, she had to press her thighs together. The excitement of being the one to seduce, to call the shots was thrilling.

"Um...you changed."

She tilted her head. "I thought I'd get into something a little more...comfortable."

His gaze traveled down her curves, over her legs, to her heels, and back up again. "I like the outfit." He grinned at her, and she relaxed some. He wasn't going to call her crazy and kick her out of his office. This was good. He smiled and even laughed a bit. That was so much better than the bear of a mood he'd been in earlier.

"Thank you," she said primly. She ran her hands down her sides as she stood straighter. "I'm ready for dick-tation, sir."

He smiled full out and tapped his pen on his notepad. "Dick-tation? Is that right?"

She nodded quickly. "Oh, yes, sir. My fingers are ready to type." She giggled, and he laughed. "Well, you know, my fingers are ready for all *sorts* of things."

"What the hell kind of porn did you watch before you came in here, Fall?"

She scowled and picked up the ruler she'd placed on his desk that morning. She wacked it against her palm a couple of times. "You know, you have to play along. I was going for sexy secretary and dirty boss, but we can do school teacher and bad adult student."

His eyes grew dark and he licked his lips. He ran a hand over his denim-clad cock and tilted his head. "Why don't you sit down and start typing. I want you to get what I'm saying word for word. You think you can do that, miss?"

She grinned then, thankful he was playing along. She needed him to smile, to laugh. She didn't want to think about why that was so important to her so she pushed it away, focusing on sitting down primly on the edge of the seat instead. She adjusted her breasts so they plumped up nicely between her arms as she typed, and Griffin snorted. She might be going for sexy, but the farce was a little much. Again, she'd take the laughter...and whatever else he gave her once her skirt was above her hips.

"Once, there was a very, very bad secretary..." Griffin started.

"Is this a new book, sir?" she asked, typing away on a blank page.

"Did I tell you to interrupt me?"

She bit her lip and glanced at him, a laugh threatening to break free. "No, sir."

"You did a very bad thing, miss. I think you're going to have to be punished."

She widened her eyes and put her hand in front of her mouth. "Oh, sir, not a *punishment*."

Griffin stood up and prowled toward her. There wasn't another word for it, not the way he moved, all grace and strength and power. She licked her lips, and he took her chin in his grip, forcing her gaze to his.

"You've been a bad girl, Fall. Stand up."

She swallowed hard and stood. Her ankles went wobbly in her heels, and Griffin gripped her hip with his casted hand.

"You okay, honey?" he whispered, not in the game.

"Just fine," she whispered back, a smile on her face.

"Good." He narrowed his eyes then stood back. "Bend over the chair, Fall, and pull up your skirt. I think you need to show me how bad you are."

She moved past him, slowly sliding her body against his as she did. She went to the side of the chair and bent over, wiggling her hips as she slid her skirt over her waist.

"Holy fuck," he whispered. "Did you forget panties this morning?" He came to her then and ran his large hand over her backside. "Actually, if I remember right, you had panties on this sweet ass of yours when you were in your yoga pants. That means you took them off for me." His fingers dipped inside her heat and she moaned. "You're wet, Fall. Is that for me?"

She looked over her shoulder as he licked his fingers and she groaned. "Jesus, Griffin. You are so sexy sometimes."

He smiled. "Only sometimes?"

"Well, sometimes you're an asshole, but I like you anyway."

He slid his hand over her ass again, squeezed. "I like you, too."

So serious.

Too serious.

Then he knelt behind her and licked her. She

gripped the edges of the chair, burying her face against the leather as he buried his face in her. He licked and sucked, his lips doing amazing things to her clit. She pressed her hips back, riding his face as he ate her out. Soon she was coming, calling out his name as her knees went weak. Griffin was there though, holding her up and keeping her close as she came down from her high.

She hadn't planned to come by his mouth right off the bat. First, she wanted to do something for him. As soon as her mind cleared, she tried to get back to her plan.

"Don't fuck me," she panted, and Griffin froze.

"What's wrong? Did I hurt you? Is it your heels?" He quickly sat on the chair and pulled her onto his lap. His cock pressed against her bare ass, and he ran his hands over her body.

Hell. She could fall in love with this man. Fall in love with the way he called her Fall, the way he cared for her when he didn't realize he was doing it. She could fall easily. And she had to pull back before she broke under that feeling.

"I'm okay, Griffin." She paused. "Better than okay. But I wanted to do something before you fucked me hard and I forgot my plan."

His shoulders relaxed and he let out a breath. "Fuck. You scared me."

She cupped his face and kissed him softly, loving the taste of herself on his lips. "I'm sorry."

He pulled back, just a little to know that he was trying to close off feelings, as well. Good. She wasn't sure what she would do if they both had to deal with those issues. Better to get back to the hot sex that meant friendship and nothing else.

"I want to have you in my mouth," she said into the silence. "Can I?"

He laughed then, a full-bodied laugh that went straight to her heart. "You want to give me a blowjob? Hell, yeah, you can suck my cock. You want me to sit here and keep my hands off you while you do it? Or will you take off that shirt of yours, keeping the skirt and heels on, of course? That way I can play with your tits as you suck me off."

She rolled her eyes and hopped off his lap. Well, hopped in the sense she wiggled off while he kept his hands on her hips so she didn't fall in her heels. He squeezed her hand before helping her to her knees, and she had to swallow hard. She wasn't supposed to be feeling anything but lust when it came to Griffin Montgomery.

She quickly took off her top, forgetting she'd planned to be slow and sexy with the buttons, and threw her bra to the floor, as well. She wanted him in her mouth, and frankly, wanted to forget anything that didn't have to do with sex. Feelings couldn't matter. He helped her undo his pants and held the base of his cock as she looked up at him through her glasses.

He reached out with his casted hand and played with the edges of her hair with his fingertips. "I didn't know I had a thing for a girl in glasses as she gave me a blowjob. Good to know."

She rolled her eyes and put her hand over his, squeezing his cock. He let out an oof and she lifted up slightly to lick the slit at the head of his dick. He moved his hands from beneath hers and went to her breasts, cupping them and playing with her nipples. She hummed as she swallowed the head of his cock before pulling back and licking up and down the shaft. She liked giving blowjobs. Liked the feeling of being in control. And she would be the one in control. At least until he tangled his hand in her hair and kept her still while he fucked her mouth. But even then, she would be the one giving him pleasure even as he took it. It was a heady and sensual power, and she wouldn't take it for granted.

When she swallowed him whole, he shuddered and did indeed slide his fingers into her hair. She kept up a steady rhythm, loving the way he groaned and called her name. She rolled his balls in her palm before sucking on each, letting them go with a popping sound. When he stiffened and groaned again, she kept him in her mouth even when he would have pulled away. The first spurt hit the back of her throat, and the rest filled her up. She swallowed each drop, her gaze on his as he came.

When he pulled away and reached for her, she leaned back, needing to catch her breath. She'd seen something in his eyes that scared her. Something that was far too close to non-just-sex. She couldn't afford to let him get closer, couldn't afford to do more than they'd already done. Perhaps she couldn't even afford that.

"Come with me to the bedroom," he whispered. "Stay the night."

She hadn't stayed over since that first night, and she wouldn't be doing it again. She couldn't.

"I have to go," she said, her voice oddly hollow. "Thank you."

She didn't know what she was thanking him for, but she stood up and grabbed her clothes, putting them on as she made her way into the living room.

"Autumn!"

"Bye!"

She left with her shoes in her hand and her bag on her shoulders. She was out of the house and in her car by the time he made it to the front door, but she didn't listen to him as he called her name. Things were getting too close, too dangerous.

And when danger came, she did what she did best. She ran.

Griffin stared at the TV but wasn't really seeing what Jake and Decker were doing with their video game. His turn would come next, but first, he had to figure out his brain. Or at least try to. His mind was on Autumn and the fact that she kept running. She'd surprised him with that outfit and role-play. He'd had fun, and had enjoyed licking her until she came. And the blowjob? Fuck. That had been the best blowjob of his life, and had popped his top faster than ever before. Maybe not since he'd been a teen.

And then she'd practically tripped over her heels to run away from him when he'd wanted to go back to the bedroom—when he'd asked her to stay the night. Why the heck had he asked her to stay the night? They were *casual*. No strings. That's what he wanted. He wasn't even sure he wanted to have a full-on relationship like his other family members had. He might have thought it was nice in some respects, but he liked things the way they were. Or the way they had been. He may not have been writing as he should, but he'd been somewhat happy. And yeah, Autumn had come and blown his routine to smithereens, but he was writing now.

He frowned, his nail scraping absently at the label on his beer bottle.

He was writing.

He was actually enjoying his job again.

He'd had a path for his character to get through the death of his girlfriend. His character Jensen had been through hell, but he was going to get through it. It wasn't going to be easy—it sure hadn't been easy for Griffin all those years ago when it came to Lauren—but it was something that could be done.

Autumn was helping him, and he had no idea what to think about that.

Jake and Decker cursed at each other as they kept up the pace on their turn of the game, and Griffin waved them off when they offered him a turn. He needed to think, needed to figure out what his next step was. Because he could either chase her down and make her come clean with her secrets, or let her walk away like she had always planned to do.

Honestly, he had no idea what he wanted.

And that scared him.

He had always known what he wanted, and one look at Fall and he had lost it.

Perhaps that wasn't quite true, though. He hadn't been able to write without her there to help his thoughts. He hadn't been able to do a lot of things. What would happen when she left? What would happen when the book ended?

She was hiding something from him, he was sure of it. But then again, he was hiding something, too. He might have told her about Lauren, but he hadn't told her about everything to do with his feelings on it. Hadn't told her about his passion for writing and how he'd almost lost it. The secrets had almost cost him this book and they still could, but he knew Autumn held more secrets than that.

If he went to her and asked her why she ran, then they'd have to talk about their relationship, and Griffin wasn't sure if he wanted to do that. He liked what they were. He liked having her in his bed when he could and getting through work with a smile on his face, even if he sometimes wanted to pull his hair out. If that changed, well...that would suck. It would also hurt what they had, and he wasn't sure what they had to begin with.

She had told him she was a nomad but hadn't told

him anything else about her life. And when he'd asked, she'd pushed him off, changing the subject. How many times could he let her do that before he gave up or pushed harder? It hurt that she wasn't completely honest with him, when he'd at least told her about some of his past. There was something hurting her, he knew it, and there was nothing he could do about it. Like with his hand, he'd broken it trying to protect her in the car accident, yet it hadn't been enough. He'd broken himself, and it had been luck that she hadn't been hurt.

She was always so scared. So skittish.

And he wanted to know why.

He needed to figure out what *he* wanted first before he peeled off her layers. Because no matter what, he didn't want to hurt her. And from the look in her eyes, she'd been hurt before.

What did he want with Autumn Minor?

And, maybe more importantly, what did she want with him?

"Hey, you okay?" Jake asked as he leaned into Griffin's shoulder.

"What's wrong?" Decker asked.

"I...I can't talk about it." He played with the label on his beer again.

"If it's Autumn, you can talk with us," Jake said

softly. "I know we joke that us guys aren't supposed to talk about relationships, but that's bullshit."

"Let us help," Decker added.

Griffin swallowed hard, shaking his head. He didn't want to betray Autumn's confidence by even voicing his concerns. She may not have told him a damn thing, but he didn't want to make her feel she *couldn't*. The fact that his friends were there to help, though? That made him feel slightly better, and part of his chest untightened ever so slightly.

"I can't," he said softly. "Yet," he added when Decker stared at him.

"Okay, then," Jake said after a moment. "When you're ready, we're here. Or, hell, any of the Montgomerys would be. Just remember that."

Griffin nodded and set down his beer. "Thanks." He cleared his throat and let thoughts of Autumn settle into the back of his mind as they were prone to. She never quite left his thoughts. And that worried him, as well. "Now, whose ass do I get to kick?" he asked as he stole Jake's controller from his hands. "I'm playing one-handed so I get extra points to start, right?"

"Asshole," Jake mumbled. "It was my turn, but whatever. Play Decker, and I'll play the loser." He winked. "Or the loserest loser."

Decker rolled his eyes and Griffin groaned. "Jesus.

We need better comebacks. We're too old to sound like eight-year-old boys playing Minecraft."

"Truth," Decker added. "And no, Griffin. You don't get extra points. You break the hand, you deal with the consequences. And the losses. Jake, go get us a couple more beers since you're twiddling your thumbs over there."

Jake flipped them off then went to the kitchen while Griffin settled into the couch. He might not know what he was going to do with Autumn, but he at least knew he had *something*. He could breathe for the moment.

And when he let the thoughts come back in full force, he'd worry about Autumn.

He would figure it out.

He had to.

CHAPTER FOURTEEN

Autumn's hands hurt from the amount of typing she'd done that day without actually speaking to Griffin beyond a murmured assent here or there. It was awkward as hell, and she didn't know how to fix it. They hadn't even kissed during their breaks.

Had she broken them?

Had he?

Hell.

She needed a hot bath.

And her bed.

Her bed sounded wonderful. Magical even.

And it had nothing to do with his bed. She would be able to breathe and enjoy the rest of her night, which would include leftover pizza and sleep. She couldn't wait. And when she did all of that, she'd ignore the fact that Griffin hadn't done anything different to her except what he *hadn't* done. He'd acted the same as always, and yet she'd wanted more from him. That was on her.

She'd run, and he'd let her.

She'd run, and now she didn't know what to do next.

Autumn hated not knowing what to do. She'd run before because of it, and people had gotten hurt. She only had herself to blame.

But maybe she didn't have to leave...maybe things were different this time.

That was the first time she'd ever thought something like that. It was dangerous.

She knew she shouldn't have run like she had when Griffin had asked her to stay the night. She'd been practically naked at the time, and running around in heels and no panties with her skirt hiked up over her hips just made her look like an idiot. An idiot with secrets to be kept. Griffin had asked her before what her secrets were, even going as far as to try and kiss them out of her, but she'd held strong. But she hadn't missed the curiosity in his eyes, the *hurt* that he felt because she wouldn't tell him.

She couldn't tell him.

He loved solving mysteries, and Autumn Minor was the greatest mystery of all.

She pulled into her driveway and grabbed her bag. It didn't surprise her that even as she'd run out of his home nearly naked and dressing quickly, she'd grabbed her bag on the way out. It was her life, her sanity. Without it and the things in her trunk, starting over once again wouldn't be nearly impossible.

Autumn groaned as she shuffled to her postage stamp of a front porch. She was just so tired. She hadn't slept the night before with thinking of Griffin and how she'd left things. Then today she'd spent most of her energy trying to act like everything was normal when it clearly wasn't.

She was so in her head that she'd almost missed the fact that her front door was cracked open. She froze, the hairs on the back of her neck rising. She calmly and methodically pulled out her pepper spray. She didn't go inside—she was smarter than that.

He could be waiting for her in there.

He could be waiting for her out here.

She quickly looked through her window since she was close enough to see, and bit her lip so she wouldn't call out. Someone had trashed her place. Her couch was on its side—ripped open with what looked like a very sharp knife. Her books and clothes were in shreds on her floor, and everything that had been in her fridge was smeared on the carpet and walls.

There would be no going back inside to get what was left of her belongings. There would be no more Denver for Autumn. She gripped her weapon in her hand, the pain from typing all day all but forgotten as her adrenaline surged. She looked over her shoulder then ran to her car.

Before, she would have gone slowly, trying to act casual, but not this time. She didn't have the strength to not call attention to herself. As it was, her neighbors obviously hadn't even noticed a strange man tearing up her house. She knew full well it could have been a robbery in this neighborhood, but her instincts were screaming to run and find a safe place. This wasn't random.

This was *him*.

Her hands shook as she unlocked her car door with the plastic fob and jumped inside. Her bag ended up underneath her in the rush, but she didn't care. She slammed her car door shut, locked them all, and had the vehicle started by her next breath. She peeled out of the driveway, at least cautious enough to look behind her in case she hit another car or something. Anything that would keep her in his presence longer couldn't happen.

She'd thrown the pepper spray on her passenger seat so she could have both hands on the wheel as she made her way down the street. Her body was shaking, and her teeth bit her lip, cutting into it. She tasted blood but ignored it. The pain kept her present and not in the past where screams and fear overwhelmed. She was stronger now than she ever was before.

Far stronger.

Her heart ached at the same time it raced. She would be leaving Denver. Leaving the Montgomerys.

Leaving Griffin.

All without so much as a goodbye. But she couldn't afford to stay. The man that had haunted her nightmares for far too long had found her and it wasn't safe to stay. She'd go somewhere warmer like she'd thought before. Denver was too cold for her anyway. It was good she was going to see new places. She'd learn so much and gain new friends—the new ones not as close, of course. She couldn't afford to have her heart break like this every time.

She licked her bit lip and winced at the taste of blood and salt from her tears. She had her forged documents in her bag and her emergency kit in the trunk of the car. With that and her almost full tank of gas, she didn't need anything else. She never did.

She didn't need anyone else.

Autumn was on the road, her mind on getting out of Denver when she realized where her subconscious had led her. Fifteen minutes, she inwardly screamed. A fifteen-minute drive, and look where it had led her.

Not to safety. Not to a far-away place where no one would know her.

But to a driveway she knew better than her own. A house she spent more time in than hers. She pulled in, but didn't let her foot off the brake, didn't put her car in park. She shouldn't be here. It wasn't *safe*. Her body shook, and tears poured down her cheeks as she tried to gain the courage to drive away, to do what she always did.

Run.

Only she didn't have the energy. She was just so *tired*. She didn't want to do this on her own anymore. But what if he'd followed her? What if he was there now, watching her in front of this house. She swallowed hard, her lip still bleeding slightly. For all she knew, the man had watched her all this time and already knew about this place. He knew enough about her to be able to trash her home when she wasn't there.

"Oh, God," she cried out. What was she going to do?

A knock on the window forced a scream out of her and her foot fell off the brake. The car lurched forward, almost hitting the garage door. She quickly pressed down on the brake again and put the car in park.

"Autumn! Unlock the door. What the hell is going on? Are you hurt?"

She shook her head, but didn't let her hands leave the steering wheel, didn't turn off the car. She needed to go. It wasn't safe here. She kept saying that over and over to herself, even as Griffin pounded on the car door.

Griffin cursed and called her name, but it was as if she could barely hear him, her mind going to her safe place. Only it wasn't safe there, not when she needed to be on the road and out of Griffin's life forever.

"I will break this window, Autumn. Open the fucking door. Now."

She turned to him, her mouth opening and closing, but she didn't say anything. Couldn't. This was what shock felt like. She'd felt it before, but it had been a while. He hadn't been this close before.

Griffin put both palms on her window and rested his head between them. "Autumn, baby. Open the door. Please. Please let me help."

She studied him. Oh, Griffin. He tried so hard. Tried to help her, and she refused to let him. It would have been better if he'd never offered, never tried. It was too hard now.

Carefully she lifted one hand from the steering

wheel and placed it on the glass mirroring his. His fingers twitched as he met her gaze, his eyes dark with worry.

"Please, baby. Please, Fall. Open the door for me. Let me in."

Let him in? Could she do that?

Let him in to see everything?

She wasn't sure she could, but she knew she couldn't drive right then. She'd hurt someone or herself if she drove in her condition. With her eyes on him, she turned off the car, watched the way his shoulders relaxed marginally. Then she unlocked the doors. Before she could open her mouth to speak, he had the door open and her in his arms.

"You weren't even wearing your fucking seatbelt, Autumn," he growled in her ear. His hands went down her body, checking for injuries it felt like. "You're bleeding," he whispered, his hand on her chin.

"I...I can't be outside." She pressed her lips together, the sting of the cut pulling her a little more out of her fog. "I need...I need..." She couldn't finish the sentence. She didn't know what she needed.

Griffin nodded then reached around her and closed her car door. "You have your bag on you still so that's something. Anything else you need out of the car?" He took her keys from her then surprised her by tucking his hand under her knees and pulling her to his chest. He carried her that way, kicking his front door shut behind him. Apparently, he'd left it open as he'd stormed out to her.

That made her heart clench, warmth spreading through her, but she tried to tamp down those feelings. It wasn't smart to feel that. She shouldn't be in his arms, shouldn't let him carry her...but it had been so long since she'd let another help her, let another take her burden.

It wasn't fair to let Griffin do that now.

He set her on the couch so carefully that she almost cried again.

"Lo-ck...lock your doors." She couldn't get the words out the first time. As it was, she was barely holding it in. Tears still fell from her eyes, but she wasn't sobbing uncontrollably. Yet.

That would come unless she got a handle on her emotions.

Griffin cupped her face and forced her gaze to his. "I'll do that, Fall. Anything else you need?"

She tried to open her mouth to say something, but she didn't know what it was. Instead, she swallowed again and let him release her. She would not feel sad at the loss of his touch. Griffin locked the door, slid the deadbolt in, and hooked up the chain. He lived in a safe neighborhood but seemed to have more security than her.

When he clicked a few buttons and the security system she didn't know he had beeped, she almost wept harder.

"You're safe in here, Autumn," Griffin said when he walked closer. "Give me a minute. I'll be right back. I promise."

She nodded, her eyes on the locked front door. There were more entries into the home, but she could feel safe at least for the moment. Right? No. She couldn't think like that. She needed to drive away and keep Griffin safe. He was more important than her. She couldn't let another person get hurt because of her.

Griffin was back before she could figure out what her next step was. He had a cup of coffee in one hand and a tumbler of amber liquid in the other. He also had a first aid kit tucked under one arm and a bottle of water under the other.

If she hadn't been crying already, she'd have started then.

This man…this man.

"I just made this pot," he said as he handed her the cup. "Though you look wired enough that maybe coffee isn't the best idea. So I have whiskey, too." She frowned.

"Good whiskey. I can even add said whiskey to the coffee if that helps."

He sat on the coffee table in front of her and sighed. "Just tell me what you need and I'll do it."

"I...I could use the whiskey," she whispered, her voice oddly hoarse. "But I can't drive after I do."

He met her gaze, his eyes pleading. "Don't drive anywhere. Not tonight." He set the whiskey down next to him along with everything else. "Please."

She licked her lips, winced when her tongue hit the cut.

"Please," he repeated.

"Okay," she whispered.

He let out a sigh then added the whiskey to her coffee—not all of it, but enough to sooth her nerves. He slammed back the rest of it before setting the tumbler down on the table.

"Let me take care of your lip," he said softly.

"I...there's nothing you can do."

He shook his head. "You don't know that." She knew they weren't talking about her lip just then.

She let him wipe down her cut and clean it. It was already healing and had stopped bleeding, but it still hurt if she touched it.

"You bit your lip, Autumn," he said, his voice smooth, overly controlled. "Can you tell me why? Can you tell me why you're as white as a sheet and shaking?"

"I can't," her voice broke and she took another sip of her whiskey-laced coffee, careful of her lip.

"You can, Autumn," he said, his voice breaking ever so slightly. "You can tell me anything."

He took the mug from her hands and cupped her face. She held back a sob.

"Autumn. Tell me. *Please*."

Her body shook and her heart raced. She'd kept everything inside for so long, never allowing another to know her thoughts, to know her feelings. No one knew her past. If they did, they could be hurt...but what if she didn't hold it in any longer.

What if she told him?

Griffin's eyes stayed on her, his face begging her as much as his words.

She didn't know what she'd say, what she'd do, and when she opened her mouth, the word she uttered surprised her. It shocked Griffin too from the way his eyes widened.

"Okay."

"Okay," he repeated on a breath. "Okay. Tell me."

She swallowed hard and pulled away from his hands. He frowned, but she took his hands in hers instead. She couldn't speak when he cupped her face.

"My name isn't Autumn Minor."

His eyes widened, but he nodded. "Okay."

God this man was so strong, so...ready to listen. She had to be ready to say it all. Reveal her truths, reveal her past.

She could do this.

"My name is Hannah Daniels." He didn't interrupt her, and she gained the courage to continue. "I...didn't exactly go about it legally when it came to changing my name." She paused.

"We can deal with that. If you're running from something that forced you to change your name, then we can deal with that."

"I hate the word running," she said softly. "I feel like I've been running all my life."

"Autumn..."

She let out a breath. He still called her Autumn, not Hannah. She liked that. She was his Autumn...if only for the moment.

"I have a brother and two parents. They loved me... they might still love me, but as I haven't spoken to them in ten years, I don't know. I left home at eighteen and never turned back. I couldn't."

She closed her eyes and took a deep breath. "I'm saying this all out of order. I should start at the beginning."

Griffin pulled away only to unscrew the bottled water and hold it to her lips. She swallowed a big gulp and nodded in thanks. He knew what she wanted before she did...

"In high school I did pretty well academically. Got all As and knew I would be going to college. I wasn't the all-star athlete or popular girl who would end up valedictorian with those grades. I was just an average good student, if that makes sense. I took the right classes and had a few friends who I hung out with. Everything was good. Not great, not bad. I didn't hate high school... until my senior year."

She took another sip of water and let Griffin run his hands up and down her thigh, comforting her.

"I had AP History with Mr. Sanders. Jeff Sanders. He was the awesome teacher with the great reputation. The one with the fantastic smile that the single moms—and some not-so-single moms—tried to flirt with. He was the one that the teenage girls and some of the teenage boys had crushes on. He was the popular one. Everybody loved Mr. Sanders."

The last part she bit out through clenched teeth, and Griffin cupped her jaw. "Baby..."

She liked when he called her baby. When he called her Fall. She just liked him.

But that wasn't what she was talking about then.

"There were always rumors about him, you know. How he slept with a couple mothers, but anyone who heard that and loved him said it must have been the slut women making up stories. It was always the woman's fault for daring to want to sleep with him. Mr. Sanders could do no wrong."

She shook her head.

"There were also rumors about him with the girls in his class, even the ones that hadn't quite reached eighteen yet. Everyone was allowed to pick their seats in his class, but for some reason, the front row was always girls. Usually girls who wore skirts. I never knew how he made that work out for himself." She shuddered. "He sat me in the front row my senior year. I loved wearing skirts, loved the way the silk felt on my legs." She sighed. "I still do. I wouldn't let him take that away from me."

Griffin squeezed her thigh. "Good."

She smiled sadly. "He paid special attention to me. I was young enough to think of it as him being a good teacher. At first. Then it became...more. He would ask me to stay after class. Would gently brush my hair back as he leaned closer. It scared me."

"That man deserves to be shot."

She rubbed his hand. "It gets worse."

"Tell me," he repeated.

"When I told my parents about it, they brushed it off." Tears filled her eyes and she blinked them back. If she started crying again, she wouldn't make it. "They brushed it off. They thought I was just making it up. This was *Mr. Sanders*. He wouldn't do that. I was just confused."

"Fuck them."

She sniffed. "Yeah, fuck them. They were wrong. Maybe they would make a different choice now, but they were wrong then."

"Fall, tell me all of it."

"He got angry when I told him I'd told my parents. One day he cornered me after school and said that I was bad. That because I had told my parents, even if they didn't believe me, that I would be punished. He had all the power and I had nothing."

"Did he touch you, Autumn? Did he hurt you?"

"He never raped me. Never touched me inappropriately. I never gave him a chance. He was obsessed with me. He left me notes, was always where I was when I went to the movies or to my job at night. He was always *there*. And no one believed me. It was all coincidence, they said. They blamed me for trying to harm a good man's reputation."

Griffin squeezed her hands. "What happened next? Why are you running?"

"The day after graduation, things went to hell. You see, when I was so scared during my last half of the semester, my grades slipped. I passed everything, but I had brought shame and humiliation to my family. I didn't go to graduation, didn't go to any parties. I just stayed at home."

She shuddered.

"That's how he found me. While my parents and brother were out to dinner as a family," she hiccupped, "he came into my home. I don't know if he wanted to kill me or...well...you know."

Griffin let out a low growl, and while that should have scared her, it settled her more than it should have.

"I hit him with a frying pan of all things. I had wanted eggs, and it was the only thing close. He came at me again, hit me until I bled. I screamed and screamed. And no one came. I hit him again with the skillet and escaped with my cell phone."

Griffin moved then, pulling her onto his lap. "Baby."

"I called the police, but the captain there was friends with Mr. Sanders. Best friends, in fact. There were things about alibis said, and the fact that I was a liar. Some said I must have hurt myself." Griffin cursed. "Others said it was a home robbery or my loser boyfriend—which I didn't have, but they all thought I must have—that'd hit me. No one could believe it was Mr. Sanders."

"I don't understand how no one would take your word for it. You had bruises, baby. They should have taken that as fact."

"They didn't. No one believed a teenage girl where a very, very smart man went against her. His reputation was intact, while mine was tarnished. I was on a scholarship for the college I had planned to go to. It was revoked on account of my...transgressions with the police, as it wasn't a full academic one but also relied on my honor."

"What the fuck?"

"Yep. Pretty shitty, huh? The thing was, even though I couldn't go to college, and my family didn't trust me like they should have, I ended up with nothing because I was damn scared. And through all of that...I wasn't safe. *He* was still there. Watching. Oh, he was different about it, you know? Much more careful. He never touched me again, but he was always *there*."

"So you ran."

She nodded. "At first it was just to get away from the looks, the fear. And after the first time he showed up at my job four states away, I knew I would never be safe unless I kept running." She let out a whimper. "I need to run again, Griffin. It's not safe for you."

"Why do you say that? For me? Fall, you're the one getting hurt each time. You're the one on the run. How am I not safe? How can I help you?"

"He hasn't hurt me since I've been running, but he's hurt others." She pressed her lips together. "Every time I get too close, others get hurt around me. Mary, a waitress I once worked with, ended up hurt because she wouldn't tell him where I was. Others have been hurt, too. I can't risk you. I need to go."

She tried to stand up, but he held her tightly on his lap. He kissed her temple, and she closed her eyes. "You're not risking me. I'll be the one to risk myself." He paused. "Why haven't you gone to the police since?"

"I need to keep running. Jeff Sanders has money and knows enough people to get what he wants. He never got caught any other time he hurt someone. He always wiggles his way out."

"You're with the Montgomerys now. You go to the police now. We won't let anything happen to you."

"I want to believe that. God, I want to. But I can't. I need to go." She kept repeating that, knowing it wasn't safe. "He was in my home tonight, Griffin. He ruined almost everything I own."

Griffin's hands tightened on her. "What? What the fuck, Autumn."

"He's here, Griffin. He's *here*."

Griffin kissed her temple again and rocked her back and forth, his body as tight as a bow. The rage coursing through him was so palpable she could almost taste it.

"We should call the cops."

"Not now." She pressed her face into him. If she called the cops, Jeff Sanders would just get angrier. That's how things worked.

"Baby."

"I...I..."

"Then move in here. You can't go home. Stay with me, Autumn. Stay until we can figure it out. Let me keep you safe."

He kissed her softly, begging her to stay. She was just so...tired. Tired of running, tired of the fear. Tired of having no one to lean on. She could stay the night, maybe another day, but then she would run again and keep him safe.

"Okay," she whispered.

Griffin squeezed her tight. "Thank you."

He kissed her again, and she leaned into him. Only for the night, she told herself. Then she would gather her courage and keep the others she cared for, keep *Griffin*, out of the line of fire.

It was all she could do.

CHAPTER FIFTEEN

Griffin kept his eyes on Autumn as she slept in his arms. She'd let him put her to bed, though she'd slept in her clothes. She hadn't wanted to be without the ability to run on a moment's notice.

It broke him that she was so scared. That this seemingly confident woman would shake and not be able to breathe because of a teacher with an obsession, made him want to scream and rage. It was more horrifying than any novel he could write, any plot he could dream up.

He wanted to fix everything for her, fix things like he had countless times before for others. But this wasn't something he could easily do. Not only was there a man out there threatening her, but she'd also forged documents and had had to lie to the police at least once that he knew of.

They could figure that out, though. He knew people on the force that he'd talked to at length during his research. Plus, he knew that she'd done what she'd done to protect herself; they weren't fully lies. There was a difference.

He'd shot off a text to Decker before he'd gone to bed next to her to spread the word through the family that they should keep a look out. He hadn't gone into detail, but after what had happened with Miranda's ex, the family knew to keep tight in times of need. He also knew he wouldn't be able to keep at least part of the events from his family once they were on a tear. Considering the way Maya and Meghan had both been texting all morning, he knew time alone with Autumn wouldn't last long.

The idea that some asshole was after her...

She made a soft groan, and he released his hold on her, unaware that he'd started to squeeze tightly at the thought of that teacher trying to harm her.

He didn't know if he loved the woman in his bed, didn't know if they had forever or if this would fizzle out once they got it out of their systems, but he knew he cared.

Autumn *mattered*.

He'd have to show that without scaring her.

She turned toward him then froze, her eyes opening quickly. "Griffin."

He leaned down and kissed her temple, brushing her hair from her face. "Fall."

She sighed, and he kissed her lips.

"Morning breath," she mumbled.

He snorted then kissed her again, this time leisurely tangling his tongue with hers. She moaned against him, her nails digging into his shoulders. He pulled away and rested his forehead on hers.

His thoughts went in a thousand directions, and he could feel hers do the same from her body language alone.

"I have toiletries you can use in the bathroom."

She blinked up at him. "I have a bag in my trunk."

He nodded, a little relieved and saddened at the same time that she had a backup plan. "I'll go get it."

Her nails dug into his arms once again.

"I'll be safe." He kissed her then took her keys from the nightstand and left her in bed, confused and a little rumpled. He wanted to put her at ease, but he wasn't sure he knew how. He wasn't as good at this as he'd like to think.

Senses on alert, he made his way out to the car, grabbed her suitcase from the trunk, and pressed his lips together at the sight of her emergency kit, extra water and rations, and countless other things in her trunk. No wonder she'd been so scared when her car had broken down. If she lost this, she'd have lost her way out. He knew the bag she kept on her person at all times was important, as well.

He couldn't comprehend what it must feel like to be this scared *all* the time.

Trivial things like cleaning up after him and helping him finish his book paled in comparison to the hell she'd lived in for a decade.

He quickly made his way back into the house with her things, taking care to set the alarm system. He found her in his bedroom, frowning over his phone.

She looked up at him as he set her back down. "You told them?" Her tone wasn't accusatory, more curious.

He went to her then and she opened her legs slightly so he could stand between them. He ran a hand through her hair, and she leaned into him.

"I didn't tell them what is going on exactly, but I *did* tell Decker to gather the troops in case this guy knows about us."

She let out a sound like a whimpering kitten, and he could have kicked himself.

"This is not your fault."

She let out a breath and seemed to gather herself.

"You're in danger because of my presence. You had to tell your family to watch their backs and keep their children close without giving them details because of me. How is that not my fault?"

He cursed and placed his hand on the back of her head, forcing her gaze to his. "I told them to be cautious. And I'm thinking that when it's time, you will tell them everything. Not the children, of course, but you know what I mean. You are *not* alone, Autumn."

"You keep calling me Autumn."

He frowned. "That's what I know you as. It's who you've become. Autumn means change. Death before rebirth. You've become a woman I know and care about. If you want me to call you Hannah, I will, but I see you as Autumn. I see you as my Fall."

Emotion ran over her eyes, and he couldn't tell what it was. He hadn't told a woman he cared about her since Lauren, and he'd been too young then to truly understand the depth of such emotion.

It should have scared him, but he was too worried about what could happen rather than what could come of letting go.

"I...I like you calling me Autumn." She pulled away from him slightly. "I hate that I'm stuttering and having trouble coming up with words. I don't like being the scared little girl."

He nodded. "Then let's get ready for the day and make breakfast. We'll figure out what the next step is on a full stomach."

She raised a brow. "You always think with your stomach."

"True. Now, let's get going." He pulled her up, kissed her hard then turned her toward the bathroom with a slight smack to her ass.

Autumn stared at him before going around him to pick up her bag and head back to the bathroom. She looked like she wanted to say something but didn't. Instead, she kept going, as if she needed to keep busy before everything crashed down. He knew how she felt. Or perhaps he was the one putting those thoughts on her.

He watched her go, his heart thudding in his chest. God, he was falling in love with her.

The big L.

Fuck.

He needed to make sure she was safe. Then he could think about more.

He quickly picked up a clean pair of jeans and went to the guest bathroom. He took the fastest shower of his life, wanting to be at least clean and ready in the kitchen when she came back. Hopefully, having coffee in her system as well as food in her belly would make her feel like she was human again. He hadn't lied when he'd said he wanted her to stay there.

Things weren't safe at her place, and he wanted her by his side. His hand curled around the handle of the pan as he forced himself to take a deep breath. He didn't know if the tension came from this caveman instinct of his that had reared its ugly head, or the fact that someone had dared to hurt her, but he wanted to throw the damn pan out the window. Of course, then he'd be out of breakfast and would scare the hell out of Autumn.

He put some bacon in the pan then got out another pan out for eggs. He wasn't the best cook, but even with one good hand and one in a cast, he could scramble eggs, fry some bacon, and make toast. That paired with coffee would have to do. Autumn could probably do better, but he wanted her to focus on healing, not feeding him.

She'd crawled her way into his heart. And he didn't know how he felt about that.

She wasn't Lauren. She wasn't sick. At least not then. Yet Autumn might leave him for a whole other reason.

He'd shielded himself from others and kept his heart safe for a reason.

"Something smells good," Autumn said as she

walked into the kitchen, her voice carefully neutral. He turned to see her, *wanting* to see her.

She wore a long skirt and a cotton top with long sleeves. The skirt billowed around her ankles, making her look like she was walking on air. She was covered from neck to foot, and yet he couldn't get enough of her.

There was something wrong with him.

This wasn't the time to be thinking about his cock, about how good she looked. He shouldn't want to peel that skirt up and fuck her hard against the counter. Instead, he should be worrying about her wellbeing. She didn't have time to be fucked; her mind should be on other things.

Or maybe they both needed exactly that, he thought as her gaze traveled up his body. He knew what she saw: a shirtless man cooking bacon in jeans and no underwear. He hadn't bothered to button all the buttons on his fly, so if she looked, she'd see the dark thatch of hair at the base of his cock.

Probably not the smartest thing to be wearing while cooking bacon.

He pushed the pan off the burner before it started to sizzle rapidly and burn his chest or other important parts of him and turned off the heat. Everything was done anyway.

"I made bacon and eggs." He cursed. "Forgot to make the toast, but we can do that now."

Autumn walked to him slowly, and he stood still, afraid any sudden movement would scare her.

"I'm not scared of you," she whispered. "You don't need to walk on eggshells. I might fear *him*. But you are not him. Not once did I ever think that." She stood on her tiptoes and kissed him once. Twice. "Thank you for taking care of me."

He wrapped his arms around her. "It was nothing." He didn't know what else to do, the helpless feeling ready to overtake him.

"It was something."

He squeezed his eyes shut tightly before opening them to meet her gaze. "I want to tell my family, Autumn. Tell the Montgomerys so they can help."

She pressed her lips together and nodded. "I can do that. You already know so it's not like I can hide it from them for long."

He shook his head. "If you wanted me to keep it a secret, I would."

"Even from your family?"

"Even from them." The truth of that startled him.

"We can tell them."

He sighed and kissed the top of her head; aware

they'd kissed and held each other more in the past few hours than they had in their entire relationship.

"We need to go to the police, Autumn."

She shook her head against his chest. "I don't want to. Please don't, Griffin."

He squeezed her harder. "Baby...Fall...we need to. I know a few people we can talk to that I talked to often when I was doing research. We won't be talking to total strangers."

"I don't know if I can."

He sighed. "Autumn."

"I don't like giving in to you like this. It's like I'm losing control."

He leaned back and tilted her head up with his fingers. "You haven't had true control in far too long. You aren't a young girl, and these guys aren't in that bastard's pocket. I don't care what he thinks he can do, but he can't come in here and hurt you. We're going to fight it. I want you to be safe. I want you to stop..." He paused. "I want you."

After a long moment, she let out a breath. "Okay. We can go. It's not like I can run for the rest of my life. But damn it, this is scary."

He kissed her then. Hard. "You're so fucking brave."

She snorted, but he kissed her again.

"So." Kiss. "Fucking." Kiss. "Brave."

She wrapped her arms around his shoulders and he cupped her ass with his hands—cast and all—lifting her into his arms.

"We'll heat up breakfast later," he mumbled and nibbled on her lips. She sighed into his mouth, and he turned to set her on the kitchen counter. She slid her leg up his back, pulling him closer to her.

They kissed greedily; soaking each other in as they explored one another's mouths, felt along each other's bodies until they were both panting with need. Griffin leaned down to bite her nipple between his teeth, pleased to find that she wore no bra beneath the cotton shirt. Hands moved quickly as they stripped off her shirt, and he had her nipple in his mouth in the next breath. Autumn's head rolled back and she tangled her fingers in his hair.

"I need this, Griffin. I need *you*."

He growled against her breast before licking across her chest and paying special attention to her other breast. Autumn's hands went from his hair to his back and then back again. They were both heated, gasping for air as he pulled away to slide his hands up her legs. When he found her bare between her thighs, he groaned.

"Did you forget to pack panties and a bra in that bag of yours?"

She shook her head. "I just want you in me."

He licked his lips and nodded. "First, I need my taste." He lifted her legs to his neck, pulled her ass to the edge of the counter then slowly rolled her skirt up.

"So pretty and pink," he whispered. "You're wet for me, Fall. I can't wait to lap up all this cream and taste you on my tongue."

"Then you'd better get to it before I play with my clit and get myself off without you."

He could have fallen on the floor right then in relief. *This* was his Autumn. Sexual, confident, and *his*. He'd do all in his power to keep her that way.

When he licked between her thighs, his beard brushing along her soft skin, she shivered. Then she pressed him closer, and he grinned before humming along her clit.

"Greedy."

"Get licking, writer boy," she panted.

"As you wish, Fall." He licked her, then nibbled on her lower lips before biting down on her clit. He lapped her up, slowly and methodically until she was coming on his face, her body shaking and her voice hoarse from screaming his name.

"Griffin." He wiped his beard on the back of his hand then stood straight, his gaze on hers. She reached out, tracing her fingers on his chest. There was a moment, a connection he couldn't quite place. This woman...it scared him how much he wanted her. That internal click that didn't make sense. He buried it for now, knowing he needed to be inside her, and then protect her before he thought about things too hard.

He didn't want to love again.

He couldn't afford to.

He could be with her in the here and now, and then once she was safe, ignore the future.

It was all he could do.

She licked her lips then helped him undo his pants.

"Condom," he muttered.

She reached into her skirt pocket rolled up on her hips and handed one to him. The woman had a plan. He had to admire her for it.

He rolled it on his length and kept his gaze on hers as he slid inside her, one hand on her hip, the other on the back of her neck. They both moaned when he was fully seated. Soon she had her hands on his back, her nails raking his body, as he pumped in and out of her.

Just sex.

No strings.

He cared for her.

But this wasn't love.

Love left. Love hurt. Love had left his brother in

pain, in rehab. Love had left one sister broken after one man. Love had left him in agony after death.

He would be with Autumn in the here and now, and then let her go when it was time. They came together as he thought about how it would feel to watch her walk away. She met his gaze, and he knew she'd seen something he hadn't wanted her to see.

Whether it was that click he would ignore, or the fact that he would watch her go, he didn't know.

He was naked and sweaty, his cock balls-deep inside the woman in front of him, and yet he did his best to keep his soul intact, to keep his barriers up. Because if he fell fully, he'd break.

And Montgomerys didn't break.

He'd protect her life, then he'd leave her alone to live it.

It was the only way.

CHAPTER SIXTEEN

Something was wrong. Something beyond the fact that the cops may have believed her but couldn't do anything at the moment.

Autumn could feel the wrongness on her skin, in her soul.

Only she couldn't quite place it.

She sighed and leaned against Griffin's kitchen counter, folding her arms over her chest. Griffin was in the office doing some revisions on his book so he could get ready to write the very last part. She loved the way the book was coming together, but she hadn't told him that. He didn't look like he wanted to hear that, only wanted to get it done so he could make sure *he* was happy with it. Maybe then she'd tell him it was the best book he'd ever written in her opinion.

The fact that she could tell he didn't want to hear it spoke volumes.

She saw more of him, saw more *about* him than she thought possible. Wasn't this supposed to be a no strings, no complications relationship? In fact, it wasn't even supposed to have the word relationship attached to it. Instead, she was living at his house, sleeping in his bed, and acting like a full-on girlfriend, or even, hell, a wife.

And yet...

And yet he hadn't looked at her.

It had been a week since she'd run from her home and into Griffin's arms. After their bout of very spicy sex on the kitchen countertop, she'd noticed that something was different. There was something in his eyes that told her he was closing himself off, protecting himself.

Or maybe trying to protect her in some weird way.

He would help her find the man following her, be by her side as she spoke to the police and dealt with the legalities of her name and running, but he wouldn't be *there*.

She shivered and tried to hold herself tighter.

When they'd gone to the police and Griffin's contacts, she'd told them everything. She'd blurted it out like some insane person, but they hadn't treated her as if she were truly insane. While they hadn't been happy that she hadn't come to them earlier, they did say they would try to help.

And Griffin had been there the whole time, holding her hand and standing strong.

He hadn't smiled at her, though. Not that it had been appropriate to smile at the time, but he hadn't winked or grinned or shown her anything other than that cool look he'd had when she'd first shown up at his place to clean.

So now she was living with him, her home cleaned up thanks to the Montgomerys after the police had been there and agreed she could take away what things were salvageable. Maya had held her close then punched her in the shoulder once Autumn had told her about her past. The Montgomerys had gathered around her just like Griffin had told her they would.

And yet Griffin was pulling away.

She was sleeping in his bed.

Working for him.

Cleaning and cooking for him.

And loving him.

Damn it.

When had she fallen in love with him? When had she taken the plunge and done something stupid like falling in love with a Montgomery.

And not just any Montgomery.

Griffin Montgomery.

The one who had told her himself that he didn't want to fall in love again because he'd done so before. He'd been so young when he lost Lauren, and it had scarred him more than he wanted to admit. And now she was freaking in love with him.

Stupid, stupid, stupid.

With a sigh, she turned to start making dinner since it would need a few hours to cook. She reached underneath the counter for a pot then went to the other counter for a frying pan and cursed. She'd been living in this house for a week, working in it for over a month, and had been dealing with his unorthodox kitchen organizing system the entire time. It didn't make sense that the seasonings were near the refrigerator and the cups near the stove. It should all be put in a way that would make sense for anyone who actually cooked more than eggs and bacon.

The thought of the last time he'd cooked that for her made her blush, and she slammed the frying pan down on the stovetop. He hadn't touched her since that morning. He'd let her sleep next to him, but there hadn't been any heated moments, no more coming on his thinking chair or shower time breaks.

She grumbled a bit more then let out a breath.

"Screw it." She went to the nearest shelf and started taking things out. She'd rearrange the damn kitchen and make it easy to use. He didn't cook much anyway, and when he did, he'd find it would be easier. *She* was the one cooking. *She* was the one doing all this shit for him when all he did was act hot and cold and confuse the hell out of her.

And if she kept her worries on her relationship with Griffin, she wouldn't worry about the fact that a man was out to get her, hunting her for the past decade. That fear would never go away, but sometimes she needed to focus on something else.

Something just as scary it seemed.

"What is all that noise? What the hell are you doing?"

She turned on her heel and dropped the package of flour in her hand. Puffs of white dust filled the air and covered her from head to toe. She coughed and looked up and winced. Griffin pinched the edge of his shirt and shook it once, another puff of flour filling the air as he did.

"You scared me!" She was angry, pissed off, heated, all that other crap that had to do with ignoring her fear and dealing with the bearded man in front of her. Of course, his beard was currently white at the moment thanks to the ill-timed flour.

If the damn man had his kitchen organized correctly before, this wouldn't have happened.

"What the fuck are you doing, Autumn?"

Always Autumn. He hadn't called her Fall since he'd come inside her on the kitchen counter. She didn't know why that hurt so much. She loved him. Damn it, why did he have to pull away now?

Of course, her loving him might have had something to do with it.

"I'm cleaning so I can cook!" She knew she was yelling, but damn it, she didn't know what she was doing.

Griffin put his hands on his hips, looked around the now flour-covered room, and raised a brow. He should not look sexy covered in flour and acting like an asshole, but apparently, she had issues.

"What's with all the noise? And I thought you'd already cleaned. You have everything out of the cupboards and on the counters. What are you doing?"

She blushed then, annoyed with herself. "Your kitchen makes no sense. So I'm organizing it."

His jaw tightened. "Why? It's *my* kitchen. You're fucking it up. I know you like things organized, but still, you're messing with my things."

Seriously? This guy. He hadn't spoken to her truly in a week, and now he was getting all ragey?

"It's my job to make sure things are working right. You let me organize other parts of your house." She didn't get why he was acting this way. Or maybe at this point, he was looking for any excuse to act like an asshole.

"Yeah, you live here, fuck me, and you work for me. I guess the lines are really blurring now."

Tears stung the back of her eyes and she took a step back, her chest hurting. Who was this? This wasn't Griffin. He *never* spoke to her like this. He'd been so damn careful around her and now this?

What. The. Fuck.

She screamed, unaware she'd been so close to the edge. "You know what? Fuck you. This isn't working out. I went to the cops and they said they would watch out for me. I can go back to my place now. They said they had a car doing patrols. I don't need to be here anymore." Her hands shook and she fisted them, forcing herself to keep in control.

Griffin's eyes widened. "You can't leave. It's not safe. That bastard is still out there."

"Well, I'm looking at a bastard right now."

"Don't you dare compare me to him, Autumn. Don't you fucking dare."

She gritted her teeth. "I didn't mean it like that. But hell, Griffin. You've been treating me like an outcast, like something you want nothing to do with since the morning after I told you everything. I hate being here when you're like this, Griffin. And if I want to organize your kitchen to help you out, then I shouldn't have the fact that you *used* to fuck me thrown in my face."

"The lines *are* blurring, Autumn. But it's not safe for you to be out there."

"If it's not safe, then I can run again. I don't need to be here." Here where it hurt. She loved him. Loved. Him. And yet she couldn't say anything. The man hadn't wanted her in his life to begin with, and now he was acting as if she were something he was forced to deal with.

She pushed past him, not wanting him to see her cry.

"Autumn. Fuck. I didn't mean what I said. I'm just stressed over this book and shit. I didn't mean it the way it sounded." He followed her as she made her way to his room.

His room.

Not hers.

Nothing was ever hers. And she had a feeling she'd never have something just hers again. She started packing, throwing things back into her emergency bag. It didn't take long, as she hadn't felt comfortable enough to fully settle in. Griffin and her past had made sure of that.

"Autumn…I overreacted." He ran a hand through his hair. Last week, she would have melted at the way his arm bunched, but she hated it just then. It just reminded her of all she couldn't have. "You don't have to go. We can make things the way they were."

She noticed he hadn't said that he wanted her there.

Just that she didn't have to go.

"It's not working for me anymore," she said woodenly. "I need to go home. Need to be independent. You wanted me to go to the police, and I did. They will take care of me." She didn't quite believe that, but staying with Griffin wouldn't work. Her heart was already close to breaking; she didn't need to shatter it.

She'd handle herself as always and run if she had to. She couldn't risk the Montgomerys more than she already had.

Griffin reached out for her, and she sidestepped him. "Thank you for letting me stay here while I caught my breath. You are close to the end of the book and have been doing well on your own. Your house is clean other than the kitchen at the moment, but I'm sure you can handle that. You should be good."

He gripped her arm, but she pulled away. "Autumn. Stay."

"I can't." Her voice broke and she pressed her lips together as she ran to her car. She kept her senses on alert in case Mr. Sanders was around, but she didn't feel him, didn't see him.

She threw her bag into her car and pulled out of the driveway as fast as she could.

Griffin stood in the doorway, his clothes covered in flour and his jaw set.

He didn't come after her. Didn't put up a hand or call her name. He just stood there. Watching her go.

She didn't cry, though it was hard not to. She needed to keep her senses on alert. Just because the officers had told her that there was no one near her home and that she should be safe, her place hadn't been safe before. It was stupid that she was going back in the first place, but damn it, she had no idea what she was doing. She'd reacted in the heat of the moment, afraid for her heart, too busy worrying about that to think and the complications that came from it.

What she *should* do was get on the open road and leave, but she'd told the officers at the station that she would stay put at least for the moment—no matter what she'd told Griffin when she was yelling.

She pulled into her place and got out of the car, her

bag in her hand. She couldn't see or feel anyone around other than her neighbors, who didn't even bother to look at her. It wasn't the best place, after all.

She'd call it hers, but even then, she couldn't think of it as such.

She opened the door with her new key. Wes and Storm had changed all her locks, and the others had helped her paint the inside again, making it ready for her landlord if and when she moved out. The smell of fresh paint filled her nostrils and she frowned.

It should have been dry by then.

The one word painted in blood-red on the wall made her freeze. Her hand tightened around her pepper spray.

MINE.

She turned toward the door, ready to run, but it was too late.

"Hannah."

She opened her mouth to scream, to call for help, for Griffin, for *anyone*, but she wasn't fast enough. He had his hand around her throat and something knocked into her head.

Darkness filled her vision, and she knew this would be the end.

All of that running, all of that fear...and it wasn't enough.

She'd been stupid, had fallen for man and let it take over her brain.

This would be the end.

Griffin could have kicked his own ass. He'd gotten angry over his own goddamn feelings and thoughts and had taken it out on Autumn. With all the shit she'd had to go through in her life, she hadn't needed to deal with his attitude. Because he got scared, because he got angry, he'd lost her.

He'd seen her in his kitchen like she belonged there, thought of her in his life when he wasn't ready, and he got scared. She was doing her fucking job, and it wasn't like her being there was unexpected. Instead of handling things like a mature adult, he'd yelled.

They must have looked like two nutcases, standing in the kitchen yelling at each other with flour coating their bodies.

It wasn't her fault he'd blown up.

And it wasn't her fault she'd run from him when he'd acted like he didn't want her. Hell, he'd been acting like that all week. So scared to have her in his life, he'd lost her anyway.

Did he love her? God, he didn't know. He thought

he could. He remembered that click in the kitchen. He was just too chickenshit to look past his fears and whatever blocked him to *know*.

But in the heat of the moment, in that damned kitchen *again*, he'd connected her work to their relationship. He might have hated her interference with his book and the way he'd worked before, but he knew she'd helped him almost finish the damn thing. Then he'd added in the fact that she worked for him and fucked him. He might as well slam his head into the wall. He was an asshole. He was a douche, and his mood wasn't an excuse for what he'd done.

Now she could be in danger because he couldn't keep his damn thoughts straight.

He'd hurt her. Made her fucking *cry* because he'd been a fucking asshole.

He didn't deserve her.

He never had.

But he still needed to go after her.

He pulled behind her car and shut off his engine. Griffin gripped the steering wheel, trying to keep his anger under control. He wasn't angry with Autumn. Far from it. He needed to get a rein on his emotions and figure out what he was going to say. First, he'd apologize—grovel if he had to. Then he'd ask her, not *tell* her, to come back home with him. He'd learned from his brothers and brothers-in-law, and knew enough not to fuck up by making demands.

He was already fucking up on his own. He didn't need those mistakes, too.

After he groveled and made sure she was safe...well, maybe he'd tell her his thoughts. Or maybe he'd try to take more time. He didn't know, but sitting out in his car like an idiot wasn't helping things.

Griffin let out a breath then made his way to her small front porch. His blood froze in his veins at the sight of her front door barely cracked open.

Fuck.

His first instinct was to run inside, but he knew it might get her hurt more than she already could be. He quickly tiptoed back to the side of the house and dialed 911.

When he explained the situation, the woman on the other end of the line ordered him to stay put and said the patrol cars would be there shortly. Only he couldn't wait that long, not when he was the one to put her in this situation in the first place. He wouldn't rush in unless he could see her, he thought. And then he knew that would be a lie too.

Autumn was in danger, and there was a chance she wasn't even there to begin with. Though to most people, the sight of an open door could mean she'd forgotten to close it, he knew her better than that. Even angry and on a tear, she wouldn't make that kind of mistake.

He went to the door and peeked through the crack, not seeing anything. Letting out a slow breath, he gently pressed the door, praying no one would see or hear.

Fuck.

She lay against the wall under the word MINE scrawled in blood-red. The bastard had tied her hands together behind her back and had also tied her ankles together. Flour still covered her, but she didn't look too hurt beyond the bruise on her temple.

Jeff Sanders would die for that bruise alone.

Knowing he was a fucking idiot for going in without a weapon, he opened the door a little more and saw an older man standing over Autumn. He had his back to Griffin and was tilting his head as if studying her.

Autumn's eyes were closed, but he could still see her chest move up and down. She was breathing. Thank God.

The man bent over, his hand out as if to brush the hair off Autumn's face, and Griffin lost it. He stormed into the house, fists drawn. Sanders didn't turn right away. Instead, he moved slowly, as if he wasn't sure what was going on.

Good.

Griffin would use that to his advantage.

He slammed his fist into the man's face. Of course, since Griffin was right-handed, he used the fist with the cast on it. Pain shot up his arm, the burn so great, even the fillings in the back of his teeth rattled.

He didn't think he'd broken the damn thing again, but he had a feeling he'd done something. Whatever. It didn't matter.

The man looked up at him from the floor, dazed, and tried to get up. He tried to kick Griffin, but Griffin just straddled the bastard.

"You ever touch her again, I'll kill you." He slammed his left fist into Sanders' jaw.

Sanders smacked at him, but Griffin didn't care. This man had dared to hurt Autumn. He'd put that bruise on her temple.

Hell.

Griffin hit him again even as Sanders got in a good kidney shot. Griffin winced but tried to brush it off.

"Griffin," Autumn whispered behind him. "Stop."

He hit Sanders one more time and the bastard passed out. Or ended up knocked out. He didn't know, nor did he care. Griffin scrambled off Sanders and crawled toward Autumn.

"Baby," he whispered. He cupped her face as he pulled the gag from her mouth. "Fall."

Tears filled her eyes, and she leaned her cheek into his palm. "You came."

"I'll always come for you."

She snorted, and he had to chuckle a laugh. "Sorry."

"I was trying to be sweet and heroic and you end up making it into a dirty joke."

"It's what we're good at," she said as he helped her out of her bindings. "Is he out?"

He looked over his shoulder and nodded. Sirens pierced the silence, but he didn't allow himself to relax, not until Autumn was fully in his arms and the bastard was behind bars.

As soon as the bindings were fully off, he had her in his lap and his mouth on hers. "Dear God, Autumn, I almost lost you." The words came out on a ragged breath, and he closed his eyes firmly, willing himself not to cry when he needed to be strong for her.

Her fingers dug into his back, and he sighed. She was okay.

She was going to be okay.

And damn it, he shouldn't have let her go.

He'd be damned if he let her go again.

CHAPTER SEVENTEEN

"Well, at least the bruise is healing," Maya said from her place on the couch. The other woman had her legs crossed in front of her, and when she wasn't pressing her lips together, she was biting them as if trying not to say what she was thinking.

Considering Maya *always* said what she was thinking—at least it seemed that way to Autumn—whatever she was holding in had to be big.

Or at least complicated.

And Autumn knew all about complicated.

Autumn pressed at the bruise as she looked into the mirror. What Maya had said was true. The mark on her temple from where Sanders had gotten too close—far too close for her liking—was healing. Considering it had only been a few days since the attack, she couldn't ask for more.

Okay, so she could ask for a whole lot more, but she wouldn't just yet.

She wasn't sure how she could.

She was too embarrassed to do anything but hide.

Autumn closed her eyes and took a shaky breath. "Have I said thank you for letting me stay at your place?"

"Not in the last hour, so I suppose it was due," Maya said dryly.

When the cops had come to take Sanders away, she'd almost broken then, in fact, she wasn't sure she hadn't. Griffin had held her on his lap and murmured sweet words—sweet words she wasn't sure she hadn't made up. It was all a mix of adrenaline, fear, and a stark relief she had never thought she'd feel.

Sanders would be in jail for a long time.

There would be no hiding behind friends and using his money to get what he wanted. The police here had actually done their jobs and found out what they needed to charge him with a whole slew of things. Attempted murder, attempted rape, kidnapping, assault and battery...and that was just the big things. The man had stalking and other threatening-related charges against him, as well.

He wasn't getting away this time.

And she hadn't even spoken to him in this last attempt.

She hadn't been able to.

By the time she'd woken up from being knocked out, Griffin was there, beating the hell out of her old teacher. And as much as she'd wanted to have Sanders out of her life permanently—have the cloying, suffocating fear out of her life permanently—she couldn't allow Griffin to have that mark on his soul.

That Montgomery deserved more than that. They all did.

After she'd been checked out by the EMTs, the Montgomerys had shown up in force. She'd never felt that kind of love, that kind of care before in her life. Her parents hadn't been hateful or cruel when she'd been growing up, but their affection was nothing like the Montgomerys.

Marie and Harry Montgomery had immediately offered to keep her with them so they could pamper her. The other Montgomerys had offered, as well.

All of them except Griffin.

He'd kissed her brow and held her tightly, refusing to let her go. She honestly didn't know if that meant he'd wanted her with him and he'd expected it a done deal, or if he was done with her in truth. And because the man refused to actually say anything, she'd stepped away and gone with the loudest of the bunch.

Maya.

She'd have gone on her own, packed up her car and headed out of Denver and out of the Montgomery's lives, but she hadn't been strong enough for that. She'd had to pretend she was strong for so long, she didn't have the energy to keep it up anymore.

While she might have wanted to stay with Griffin, she knew she couldn't. Not when she was so uncertain about them and her life in general.

Due to the circumstances of her name changes, she'd gotten away with the questionable legalities of her running with only a slap on the wrist. She didn't know if it was luck or the Montgomery lawyer who had helped. The Montgomerys might own businesses, but they were still pretty blue-collar, so it surprised her the power they held. But from the way they adopted friends and family and their overall demeanor, she shouldn't have been surprised in the slightest.

"You're frowning," Maya said, pulling Autumn from her thoughts. "I didn't mean to make you feel bad about saying thank you. It's just you don't have to say it at all. I know you're grateful. But honestly, you being here helps me keep my mind off things, so it's a win-win."

Autumn turned slowly, her head tilted. "What things?"

Maya pressed her lips together and shook her head. "It's nothing."

"Maya."

"Nothing I want to talk about, okay? So let's talk about you. What are your plans?"

Autumn sighed and moved toward the loveseat, sinking into the cushions as she tried to come up with what to say. She didn't even know her own thoughts, how was she supposed to have this make sense to Maya?

"I don't know my plans," she said honestly. "I've been going from place to place, job to job for so long, I don't even remember what I wanted to do before this all started."

"You left when you were still a teenager, Autumn. Most don't know what they plan on doing at that point anyway." Maya frowned. "I'm calling you Autumn, but should I be calling you Hannah now? I mean, Sanders is gone for good, and you can go back to who you were. Right?"

Autumn shook her head. This was one thing she knew for sure—she could never go back to who she was.

"I'm Autumn now. Hannah doesn't exist anymore.

I'm going to get it legally changed, rather than how I did it before."

Maya let out a breath then clicked her tongue ring against her lip. "Good, because with that hair and your overall attitude, you're more of an Autumn to me."

She smiled. "I feel like an Autumn. As for what I'm going to do? I thought about going home." She frowned. "No, not home, that's not what it is. I guess I should call it back to where my parents live. I haven't talked to them in ten years, but I've done my best to keep up-to-date on them even in little parts. So I know they still live there. I know my brother is married and has a child."

And she'd missed all of that.

But they hadn't believed her.

They hadn't protected her.

"Damn. That sucks." Maya blew out a breath. "That really sucks. I hate that they weren't there for you. I know my family has its own drama, God do we have our drama, but we've never pulled away like they did with you. Even with Alex, we're still there for him. He might not let us get too close, but we're like piranha, we'll surround him if needed."

"Now that's an image," Autumn said with a smile.

Maya grinned. "Isn't it? And as for you, you don't

have to go back to the place you grew up. But are there any other places that call to you?"

Autumn studied her friend. There was something about her voice that told Autumn that Maya wasn't too keen on her moving away. There wasn't much she could do about that, though. Not when she didn't know her next step.

She may as well tell Maya everything. Well, not *everything*. Maya had done well with not asking about Griffin. In fact, the man's name hadn't been mentioned once since she'd been staying at Maya's. Oddly enough, neither had Jake's...

They really were a pair.

"I packed my bags this morning," Autumn finally said.

"I know. I heard you. What I want to know is why you feel you need to leave? Are you going back to your place? Because, I've got to tell you, that fucking street sucks. First, Meghan lives there after the divorce, and she and Luc almost die, then you have to deal with that shit there. No thanks."

"To be fair, our pasts came back to bite us in the ass both of those times. It wasn't actually the neighborhood."

"Technicality. But why are you leaving, Autumn? Why can't you stay? You know you'd always have a job with Montgomery Ink. I mean, hell, we need you at this point more than you need us."

Again, they didn't mention that she'd worked for Griffin mostly for the past few weeks. But Griffin didn't need her anymore. She'd gotten him in shape, and then he had told her the lines were blurred.

"I've been running for ten years."

"And you don't have to run anymore."

"But I haven't stayed in one place for so long. I've gotten used to seeing new places, seeing new people. I'm not a settler. Right?"

"Are you asking me? Because from where I'm sitting, it sounds like you're running again."

"Maya."

"Autumn."

The doorbell rang, and Maya stood up, her eyes on Autumn. "We're not done here. I know you're an adult and can do what you want, but we're going to talk about your leaving before you go. You're one of ours now, even if you don't think so."

With that, the other woman went to the front door, and Autumn put her head in her hands. She was so damn confused. She'd been trying to be someone else, hide who she was for so long, she'd forgotten who she could be. And yet, did it matter?

The idea of being with Griffin scared her more than

she could admit. Could she rely on another, could she be with him? She wasn't sure, and because of that, she had to push him away. It wasn't fair to him or his family to try and be with him when she wasn't sure who she was without him let alone who she was *with* him.

"Autumn."

She lifted her head and froze.

"Griffin."

He stood in front of her chair, his beard out of control and his hair looking as if he'd run his hands through it so much that it stood on end. He wore old jeans and a pair of boots plus a Henley that molded to his muscles. Damn man shouldn't look so good when she looked as if she hadn't slept in days.

Which was true. Tossing and turning while thinking about men in shadows and what to do about a certain Montgomery didn't allow for much sleeping.

Maya was nowhere to be found. Traitor.

"I know I should have called before coming over here, but every time I picked up the phone, I was worried you'd hang up on me."

She frowned. "What do you mean?"

He sat down on the coffee table in front of her. "Fall, baby, I pushed you away that day. I was a fucking idiot and hurt you because I was too damned scared to do anything about what I was feeling. If I had told you that I was falling for you, that at the same time the idea of you in my home and in my bed scared me as much as it made sense, you might have run away anyway. And because I was an asshole who pushed you out, you ran home to a place you got hurt. If I hadn't done what I did, you wouldn't have been in that house alone. You wouldn't have been hurt. That man got ahold of you because I let you leave. Because I didn't come after you until it was almost too late. I will never forgive myself for that. Never."

She reached out and cupped his face, his beard brushing her palm. She immediately wanted to take her hand back. Touching him was a mistake. Walking away would be that much harder.

"I am so sorry, Autumn. Forgive me. I love you," he whispered. "I love you so fucking much. You saved me, Fall. You saved me from myself, from my doubts and pains. And I know that isn't the basis for love. Fuck, it isn't with me anyway. I love you for more than that. I love the way you smile, the way you dance around the house when no one's looking. I just fucking love you. Be with me, Autumn. Come back home."

She sat still, her brain going in a thousand directions. She lowered her hand, shaken. He couldn't love her. He couldn't. She didn't even know who she was, *where* she was. How could he love someone he didn't know?

"I...I barely know who I am, Griffin. How can you love someone who doesn't even have a real name yet?"

He shook his head then cupped her face. "You're my Fall. You're my heart. I love you, Autumn. You might have a new name, might have had to run for far too long, but I know you. I know that you love helping people, that your passion is with others, not only yourself. You are so confident in other ways. I wish you would be confident here. I wish you saw what I saw."

"My bags are packed, Griffin. I'm so used to going from place to place, I figured I could find someplace else to settle if that's what I choose to do." Not quite a lie, but close enough. She was running again, only not from a man that could hurt her body, just her soul.

She was breaking, falling for a man she'd already fallen for. God, she was a coward. But what if he woke up and figured out he'd only loved her because she was there. He still had Lauren in his heart, not *her*. Her self-doubt screamed at her, saying she wasn't good enough, that she would always be the one who lied, who ran.

"I was never meant to stay," she whispered.

Griffin's eyes darkened and his face paled. "I will never force you to stay," he said slowly, his voice hoarse. "I will never clip your wings."

She shook, her hands tightened on his thighs. When had she touched him? Why was she still doing so? She had to run before it hurt more.

She had to run.

"I need to go."

"Before you do, you have to know that my HEA, my Happy Ever After, is you. It needs you. You are my future. I know that. Even if I have to run with you." He pulled back and lifted his Henley to reveal fresh ink on his skin.

"What? What is that?"

"It's the end of my book. Our book. I found my future, my words. Because of you." The elegant script was still new, so freshly inked he still wore the ointment on top of it.

"You are my destiny. My path less taken. You are my future. My home. You are my life."

"My words are written on my skin, my heart. They're in ink and memories. Love me and let me love you. Be with me until we turn our final page."

Leave it to a writer to break her into a million pieces with words of hope and love.

Tears fell from her cheeks and she leaned into him. "Griffin."

"My Fall. I've fallen for you, Autumn. I fell, and I will fall each day until the day I die. Be with me. Take a chance. Stop running and be with me."

"I love you," she whispered. The words came out of her mouth without her acceptance, but once they were said, she knew it was the truth, the one thing she should have said in that kitchen. "I'll stay."

And it was the truth. She'd stay. Not because he wanted her to, but because she wanted to. She'd been too scared to admit that. So scared she'd almost lost everything she'd thought to never have.

"Oh, thank fuck," Griffin said roughly then brought her close to him. "I am so fucking happy you love me too. I would have gone anywhere with you, and I still can. You want to go on a road trip? We can. I can write in the car, in a hotel, on a rock in the middle of nowhere. As long as I'm with you, I can write. I promise you that. But I don't know if I can do that if you're not here." He winced. "I don't mean that I need you only for writing..."

She put her fingers over his mouth. "You were doing wonderfully with the words. Let's just stop while we're ahead."

He nibbled on her fingertips. "Love you, Fall."

"Love you, writer boy. And I'll stay, Griffin. For you. For me. For us. No more running."

Griffin smiled then, and she fell in love with him once more. He brought her into his arms and she sat on his lap, straddling him. He kissed her, his mouth exploring hers as if he hadn't kissed her before yet knew every inch of her like he was part of her soul. His tongue tangled with hers and she sighed into him.

"I've missed your taste," he growled.

"I've missed you."

"I've never clip your wings," he repeated. "I'll never force you to stay."

"I'm staying because of me. Of you. Of what we could be. What we are. I'm staying because I love your family and I love this city. I've found a home, Griffin. A real home."

"Live with me. Be mine. Let us write the next page together."

This man. *Her* man. He had a way with words, a way to make her want to stay and never leave.

"Yes."

He kissed her then, and she moaned. This was their future. Their forever.

She couldn't wait to turn the page.

EPILOGUE

Griffin cupped her breasts, pushing them together and grinning like a fool.

"Are you going to just stare at my boobs or do something with them?" Autumn asked. She lay under him, naked and all rosy from coming from his mouth a few minutes before.

He sat straddled over her, his dick hard and ready. But first, he wanted to play with her tits. He loved her tits. When he bent down and licked her nipple, she let out a little fluttery sigh that told him she enjoyed his loving of her tits. A win all around.

He sucked on her, nibbling and grazing with his teeth. Her hands trailed up and down his back, starting off lazy and slow before ramping up to nails and need.

"Griffin. I swear to God, if you don't get inside me

right now, I'll put my fingers on my clit and get myself off. Without you."

"Greedy." But he shifted so his cock pressed against her cunt. They were going without condoms today. A first for them. He couldn't wait to feel her bare around him. "Ready?" He rocked his hips slowly so his dick slid along her wetness and over her clit.

"Griffin!" She reached between them but he gripped her wrists.

"Let me," he said, his voice low. Then he rocked back slightly farther before slowly entering her. They both groaned when he slid fully inside. "Jesus. Never again will we use condoms. I want to be bare inside you every single fucking day. Every day. Got me?"

"I might get a little sore, but hell yeah. Just move, okay? Fuck me hard, soft, I don't care. Just fuck me."

"My Fall, such a dirty, dirty girl. Love it."

"Love you," she said with a smile.

He watched her eyes roll to the back of her head as he moved. He started slow, then moved faster and faster until they were both gasping. Mouths meshed, sweat-slick bodies pressed against one another, hands and limbs reaching for each other. He kept his gaze on Autumn's as they made love. Her mouth parted and her eyes darkened.

"Griffin."

"I know. I know." He kissed her hard. "I love you." He pounded into her one last time and came on a roar. Her pussy clenched around him and she screamed his name. He held her close and rolled to his side, pressing kisses to her lips, her neck, behind her ear.

"My Fall."

"You have moves, writer boy," she grinned sleepily. "That is one way to wake up."

"We need to wake up every day like that."

She giggled. "Sounds good to me. Though I think I might be late to work."

He nibbled on her neck. "I know the boss. It's okay."

She pushed at him, but there was laughter in her eyes. "I'm not working for you today, remember? I'm the new Montgomery Ink receptionist."

He let out a pout but kissed her anyway. "That's right. I forgot once I was inside you. Thank God you're helping them. They are organized when it comes to everything except that damn computer."

She laughed, and he ran his hands through her hair, unable to stop touching her. He couldn't believe he had this woman, this piece of his future in his bed. And she would never leave. This was their reality, and he'd never been so damn happy.

He may write fiction, but his truth, his life, was better than anything he could put down on paper.

They were living together, taking each day at a time. He hadn't proposed yet. He would, but not now. Though it might have felt like they'd been together for years, it honestly hadn't been that long. They would take their time to get to know one another even more than they already had, and then they would take the next step. She would wear his ink though, the Montgomery Ink brand because she was one of them even if she didn't have the name yet. That was something Maya had insisted on, and he was damn well happy with it.

Things were going to be okay. It wasn't easy living in the real world and not in the fictional one of books. People didn't automatically fall in love and stay that way. They would have to work hard to make sure they were open and honest with one another. She would always have her fears, and so would he, but they could work with them, rather than hide from them.

They hadn't approached the idea of contacting her family but it would happen. She needed time to come to her new reality before she faced her old one. He understood that and he'd been honest when he said he wouldn't clip her wings. If she found that she needed to be near the family she'd run from all those years ago, he'd follow. He'd leave Denver and everything he had built here. It would hurt, but he could do it.

Autumn was *it* for him.

She'd helped him find his voice, his worlds, his confidence.

He'd finished his fucking book because of her. She would settle here with him, but never staid. They were one, they were individual, they were Fall and Writer Boy.

They were *them*.

Griffin brought Autumn closer and kissed her brow. "You take my breath away."

She fluttered her eyelashes up at him then kissed his bearded jaw. "You are the reason I feel safe to stay, feel safe to be *me*. You're my Griffin as I'm your Fall. I want to do this every morning. Every day."

He kissed her then, putting everything he couldn't say, couldn't put into words into the kiss. It didn't matter that he made words for a living; that putting those words on paper created the worlds his mind chose to live in. The woman in his arms was the reason he could write, could find the words at all. He would be able to do it on his own eventually, that was what made his Fall perfect for him, but she helped him stay true—and he knew he did the same for her.

Whatever came next for them and the Montgomerys, he knew he'd have his Fall, his Autumn by his side. He would write their journey, the course of their fate. And he'd do it with the woman whose name meant change in his life.

Griffin Montgomery hadn't been looking for love, but it had found him.

In the end, being in love wasn't a terrible thing, after all.

It was just right.

THE END

Want more ink? Coming next in the Montgomery Ink Series:

The next Montgomery finds their future in not one, but *two inked* bad-boys.

Maya, Jake, and Border's story is Ink Enduring!

&

Hailey and Sloane finally have their long-awaited romance in Hidden Ink

A NOTE FROM CARRIE ANN

Thank you so much for reading **WRITTEN IN INK!** These two surprised me and I love them! The next Montgomery finds their future in not one, but *two inked* bad-boys. Maya, Jake, and Border's story is Ink Enduring!

And as a bonus, Hailey and Sloane finally have their long-awaited romance in Hidden Ink.

Montgomery Ink Denver:
  Book 0.5: Ink Inspired
  Book 0.6: Ink Reunited
  Book 1: Delicate Ink
  Book 1.5: Forever Ink
  Book 2: Tempting Boundaries

A NOTE FROM CARRIE ANN

Book 3: <u>Harder than Words</u>
Book 3.5: <u>Finally Found You</u>
Book 4: <u>Written in Ink</u>
Book 4.5: <u>Hidden Ink</u>
Book 5: <u>Ink Enduring</u>
Book 6: <u>Ink Exposed</u>
Book 6.5: <u>Adoring Ink</u>
Book 6.6: <u>Love, Honor, & Ink</u>
Book 7: <u>Inked Expressions</u>
Book 7.3: <u>Dropout</u>
Book 7.5: <u>Executive Ink</u>
Book 8: <u>Inked Memories</u>
Book 8.5: <u>Inked Nights</u>
Book 8.7: <u>Second Chance Ink</u>
Book 8.5: Montgomery Midnight Kisses
Bonus: Inked Kingdom

If you want to make sure you know what's coming next from me, you can sign up for my newsletter at www.CarrieAnnRyan.com; follow me on twitter at @CarrieAnnRyan, or like my Facebook page. I also have a Facebook Fan Club where we have trivia, chats, and other goodies. You guys are the reason I get to do what I do and I thank you.

Make sure you're signed up for my MAILING LIST so

A NOTE FROM CARRIE ANN

you can know when the next releases are available as well as find giveaways and FREE READS.

Happy Reading!

ALSO FROM CARRIE ANN RYAN

The Montgomery Ink Legacy Series:
Book 1: Bittersweet Promises (Leif & Brooke)
Book 2: At First Meet (Nick & Lake)
Book 2.5: Happily Ever Never (May & Leo)
Book 3: Longtime Crush (Sebastian & Raven)
Book 4: Best Friend Temptation (Noah, Ford, and Greer)
Book 4.5: Happily Ever Maybe (Jennifer & Gus)
Book 5: Last First Kiss (Daisy & Hugh)
Book 6: His Second Chance (Kane & Phoebe)
Book 7: One Night with You (Kingston & Claire)
Book 8: Accidentally Forever (Crew & Aria)
Book 9: Last Chance Seduction (Lexington & Mercy)
Book 10: Kiss Me Forever (Brooklyn & Reece)
Book 11: His Guilty Pleasure (Dash & Aly)

Book 12: Maybe it's You (Riley & Gage)
Book 13: Kiss Me in the Morning

The Cage Family

Book 1: The Forever Rule (Aston & Blakely)
Book 2: An Unexpected Everything (Isabella & Weston)
Book 3: If You Were Mine (Dorian & Harper)
Book 4: One Quick Obsession (Hudson & Scarlett)
Book 5: Pretend it's Forever (Sophia & Carson)
Book 6: Wish it Were You (Flynn & Luna)
Book 7: Only Half Without You (James & Emery)
Book 8: Time Stands Still (Theo & Nina)

Ashford Creek

Book 1: Legacy (Callum & Felicity)
Book 2: Crossroads (Bodhi & Kiera)
Book 3: Westward (Atlas & Elizabeth)
Book 4: Patience (Teagan & Rush)
Book 5: Watershed
Book 6: Expanse

Clover Lake

Book 1: Always a Fake Bridesmaid (Livvy & Ewan)
Book 2: Accidental Runaway Groom (Jamie & Sharp)

ALSO FROM CARRIE ANN RYAN

Book 3: His Practically Fake Proposal (Galen & Addy)

The Wilder Brothers Series:
Book 1: One Way Back to Me (Eli & Alexis)
Book 2: Always the One for Me (Evan & Kendall)
Book 3: The Path to You (Everett & Bethany)
Book 4: Coming Home for Us (Elijah & Maddie)
Book 5: Stay Here With Me (East & Lark)
Book 6: Finding the Road to Us (Elliot, Trace, and Sidney)
Book 7: Moments for You (Ridge & Aurora)
Book 7.5: A Wilder Wedding (Amos & Naomi)
Book 8: Forever For Us (Wyatt & Ava)
Book 9: Pieces of Me (Gabriel & Briar)
Book 10: Endlessly Yours (Brooks & Rory)

The Falling for the Cassidy Brothers Series:
(Formerly the First Time Series)
Book 1: Good Time Boyfriend (Heath & Devney)
Book 2: Last Minute Fiancé (Luca & Addison)
Book 3: Second Chance Husband (August & Paisley)

Montgomery Ink Denver:
Book 0.5: Ink Inspired (Shep & Shea)
Book 0.6: Ink Reunited (Sassy, Rare, and Ian)

ALSO FROM CARRIE ANN RYAN

Book 1: Delicate Ink (Austin & Sierra)

Book 1.5: Forever Ink (Callie & Morgan)

Book 2: Tempting Boundaries (Decker and Miranda)

Book 3: Harder than Words (Meghan & Luc)

Book 3.5: Finally Found You (Mason & Presley)

Book 4: Written in Ink (Griffin & Autumn)

Book 4.5: Hidden Ink (Hailey & Sloane)

Book 5: Ink Enduring (Maya, Jake, and Border)

Book 6: Ink Exposed (Alex & Tabby)

Book 6.5: Adoring Ink (Holly & Brody)

Book 6.6: Love, Honor, & Ink (Arianna & Harper)

Book 7: Inked Expressions (Storm & Everly)

Book 7.3: Dropout (Grayson & Kate)

Book 7.5: Executive Ink (Jax & Ashlynn)

Book 8: Inked Memories (Wes & Jillian)

Book 8.5: Inked Nights (Derek & Olivia)

Book 8.7: Second Chance Ink (Brandon & Lauren)

Book 8.5: Montgomery Midnight Kisses (Alex & Tabby Bonus(

Bonus: Inked Kingdom (Stone & Sarina)

Montgomery Ink: Colorado Springs

Book 1: Fallen Ink (Adrienne & Mace)

Book 2: Restless Ink (Thea & Dimitri)

Book 2.5: Ashes to Ink (Abby & Ryan)

Book 3: Jagged Ink (Roxie & Carter)
Book 3.5: Ink by Numbers (Landon & Kaylee)

The Montgomery Ink: Boulder Series:
Book 1: Wrapped in Ink (Liam & Arden)
Book 2: Sated in Ink (Ethan, Lincoln, and Holland)
Book 3: Embraced in Ink (Bristol & Marcus)
Book 3: Moments in Ink (Zia & Meredith)
Book 4: Seduced in Ink (Aaron & Madison)
Book 4.5: Captured in Ink (Julia, Ronin, & Kincaid)
Book 4.7: Inked Fantasy (Secret ??)
Book 4.8: A Very Montgomery Christmas (The Entire Boulder Family)

The Montgomery Ink: Fort Collins Series:
Book 1: Inked Persuasion (Jacob & Annabelle)
Book 2: Inked Obsession (Beckett & Eliza)
Book 3: Inked Devotion (Benjamin & Brenna)
Book 3.5: Nothing But Ink (Clay & Riggs)
Book 4: Inked Craving (Lee & Paige)
Book 5: Inked Temptation (Archer & Killian)

The Promise Me Series:
Book 1: Forever Only Once (Cross & Hazel)
Book 2: From That Moment (Prior & Paris)
Book 3: Far From Destined (Macon & Dakota)

ALSO FROM CARRIE ANN RYAN

Book 4: From Our First (Nate & Myra)

The Whiskey and Lies Series:
Book 1: Whiskey Secrets (Dare & Kenzie)
Book 2: Whiskey Reveals (Fox & Melody)
Book 3: Whiskey Undone (Loch & Ainsley)

The Gallagher Brothers Series:
Book 1: Love Restored (Graham & Blake)
Book 2: Passion Restored (Owen & Liz)
Book 3: Hope Restored (Murphy & Tessa)

The Carr Family Series:
(Formerly the Less Than Series)
Book 1: Breathless With Her (Devin & Erin)
Book 2: Reckless With You (Tucker & Amelia)
Book 3: Shameless With Him (Caleb & Zoey)

The Fractured Connections Series:
Book 1: Breaking Without You (Cameron & Violet)
Book 2: Shouldn't Have You (Brendon & Harmony)
Book 3: Falling With You (Aiden & Sienna)
Book 4: Taken With You (Beckham & Meadow)

The Campus Roommates Series:
(Formerly the On My Own Series)

Book 0.5: My First Glance
Book 1: My One Night (Dillon & Elise)
Book 2: My Rebound (Pacey & Mackenzie)
Book 3: My Next Play (Miles & Nessa)
Book 4: My Bad Decisions (Tanner & Natalie)

The Ravenwood Coven Series:
Book 1: Dawn Unearthed
Book 2: Dusk Unveiled
Book 3: Evernight Unleashed

The Aspen Pack Series:
Book 1: Etched in Honor
Book 2: Hunted in Darkness
Book 3: Mated in Chaos
Book 4: Harbored in Silence
Book 5: Marked in Flames

The Talon Pack:
Book 1: Tattered Loyalties
Book 2: An Alpha's Choice
Book 3: Mated in Mist
Book 4: Wolf Betrayed
Book 5: Fractured Silence
Book 6: Destiny Disgraced
Book 7: Eternal Mourning

ALSO FROM CARRIE ANN RYAN

Book 8: Strength Enduring
Book 9: Forever Broken
Book 10: Mated in Darkness
Book 11: Fated in Winter

Redwood Pack Series:
Book 0.5: An Alpha's Path
Book 1: A Taste for a Mate
Book 2: Trinity Bound
Book 2.5: A Night Away
Book 3: Enforcer's Redemption
Book 3.5: Blurred Expectations
Book 3.7: Forgiveness
Book 4: Shattered Emotions
Book 5: Hidden Destiny
Book 5.5: A Beta's Haven
Book 6: Fighting Fate
Book 6.5: Loving the Omega
Book 6.7: The Hunted Heart
Book 7: Wicked Wolf

The Elements of Five Series:
Book 1: From Breath and Ruin
Book 2: From Flame and Ash
Book 3: From Spirit and Binding
Book 4: From Shadow and Silence

ALSO FROM CARRIE ANN RYAN

Dante's Circle Series:
- Book 1: Dust of My Wings
- Book 2: Her Warriors' Three Wishes
- Book 3: An Unlucky Moon
- Book 3.5: His Choice
- Book 4: Tangled Innocence
- Book 5: Fierce Enchantment
- Book 6: An Immortal's Song
- Book 7: Prowled Darkness
- Book 8: Dante's Circle Reborn

Holiday, Montana Series:
- Book 1: Charmed Spirits
- Book 2: Santa's Executive
- Book 3: Finding Abigail
- Book 4: Her Lucky Love
- Book 5: Dreams of Ivory

The Branded Pack Series:
(Written with Alexandra Ivy)
- Book 1: Stolen and Forgiven
- Book 2: Abandoned and Unseen
- Book 3: Buried and Shadowed

ABOUT THE AUTHOR

Carrie Ann Ryan is the New York Times and USA Today bestselling author of contemporary, paranormal, and young adult romance. Her works include the Montgomery Ink, Redwood Pack, Fractured Connections, and Elements of Five series, which have sold over 3.0 million books worldwide. She started writing while in graduate school for her advanced degree in chemistry and hasn't stopped since. Carrie Ann has written over seventy-five novels and novellas with more in the works. When she's not losing herself in her emotional and action-packed worlds, she's reading as much as she can while wrangling her clowder of cats who have more followers than she does.

www.CarrieAnnRyan.com

www.ingramcontent.com/pod-product-compliance
Lightning Source LLC
LaVergne TN
LVHW011758060526
838200LV00053B/3626